Adv~ ~ ~ ~ ~ ~ ~ ~ ~ ~ ~ jor

A Face on the Flag

"My friend and fellow military veteran, Kevin Horgan, provides an evocative perspective on how PTSD significantly impacts not only the veteran but those around them. Kevin's perspective has been gained from his military service and extensive volunteering in the military."

Lloyd Knight, VETLANTA President
USAF First Sergeant (ret)

"Horgan's third novel doesn't disappoint and is compelling in its reflections of the central character, a Marine veteran who believes he is unworthy of his success and doubts his potential for redemption."

Jim "Hondo" Haldeman, LtCol USMC (ret)
American Airlines 737 Captain (ret)

"Horgan's characters epitomize countless veterans' losses: lost loves, lost jobs, lost limbs. Despair and unworthiness are evident, but esprit de corps still burns within, as does potential for redemption."

Mark Frampton, Colonel USMC (ret) Owner,
Frampton Construction & The Pitchers Plank
www.pitchersplank.com

"Kevin Horgan's unique experience and perspectives gives him the ability to craft some of the most engaging and impactful stories I can find. Since his 2013 novel, *"The March of the 18th,"* his work has continued to delight!"

Jason Smith, US Air Force Veteran
City Leader for Bunker Labs Atlanta

"Horgan's novel is excellent and a reason to get this book, but his generous mission is outstanding and a better reason to get one for a friend. His mission tells you all you need to know. Bravo Zulu."

Jared Ogden
Former US Navy SEAL, CEO of Triumph Systems

"For patriotic Americans who never served in our military, the characters in *A Face on the Flag* help us appreciate the challenges, sacrifices and dedication of those who did. May God bless the men and women of our great military."

PF Whalen
TheBlueStateConservative.com

"Kevin Horgan is a great supporter of other veterans. He writes from his personal experiences and insight with a touch of humor. If you are a Patriot, you will enjoy this yarn about military friends who are the essence of successful transition from the military. Looking forward to this new novel from a man who loves his craft."

Dr. Amy Stevens, Ed.D., LPC
U.S. Navy Veteran
Founder, Georgia Military Women

"What shapes the relationships of veterans? Horgan tells us their stories, their challenges, and their friendships, all woven into a tight novel. Giving half of his royalties to support veterans is a nice bonus."

Patrick O'Leary, USMC veteran
Board Member, Hershel "Woody" Williams
Medal of Honor Foundation

"Crisp and darkly optimistic. I have known these characters in many venues in the experiences of a lifetime. Well drawn throughout. Horgan gives half his royalties away and that is another good reason to get this book!"

Brian Arrington, M.S. USAF (ret)
Founder/President VETS2INDUSTRY
#How_Can_I_Help? #Pay_It_Forward

"Is it possible to muster sympathy for a flawed veteran? Horgan's novel challenges both his well-drawn characters and the reader to decide. Veterans will see themselves in the character portraits drawn here, for good or ill."

Steve Cote, Colonel USMC (ret)

"Kevin has done it again. A masterpiece which shows how soldiers, sailors, and Marines set aside squabbles, share with each other the hardships and dangers, and assist in bearing each other's burden."

Ed DeVos, LtCol US Army (ret)
Author of *The Last 100 Yards*

"A novel that needs to be read beyond the military community. Active duty, veteran, or civilian who has had to deal with depression, racism, loss of a job, a severe injury or just the day to day struggles of life can relate to the characters in **A Face on the Flag** and come away inspired that they are not alone in their fight."

Frank Morris, Entrepreneur,
Remedium Life Science of Georgia
Georgians Committed to Patient Access

And for Previous Books...

The March Of The Orphans
And The Battle Of Stones River
(pub. 2015)

"Good historical fiction should make it a challenge for the reader to discern the difference
between actual and imagined events, creating a
cohesive narrative that enhances our connection
with the past.

***The March of the Orphans and the Battle of
Stones River*** does just that for those wanting to
take a fresh look at the Battle and the famed First
Kentucky Brigade.

Horgan has written a compelling account that
reminds us of the thousands of human stories
playing out while the battle raged on. Readers
who prefer a good story and historians alike will
enjoy this book."

Jim Lewis, Park Ranger,
Stones River Battlefield National Park,
Murfreesboro, Tennessee

The March Of The 18th,
A Story Of Crippled Heroes In The Civil War
(pub. 2013)

"Horgan expresses the emotional turmoil, the isolation, and the sense of hopelessness of those overwhelmed by physical and emotional disabilities. *The March of the 18th* is a very well written and insightful work by an author who understands so much more than is expressed in deployed morning reports."

Gerald R. Tuttle, PhD, Colonel USAF (ret)
25- year psychotherapist

"A little-known piece of American history that should be taught in our schools. Three cheers for the courage of the Veterans Reserve Corps, and *The March of the 18th*!"

Zellie Orr, Lecturer and Author of *First Top Guns, An Account of the "Last Hurrah" of the Segregated 332nd FG* (aka Tuskegee Airmen)

"Courage, leadership, and loyalty are just a few words that describe the group of characters in this Civil War story."

Don Bonsper, LtCol USMC (ret),
Author of *Vietnam Memoirs, My Experiences as a Marine Platoon Leader* (Two Volumes)

A FACE on the FLAG

KEVIN HORGAN

XULON PRESS

Xulon Press
2301 Lucien Way #415
Maitland, FL 32751
407.339.4217
www.xulonpress.com

A Face on the Flag
By Kevin Horgan

Printed in the United States of America

Paperback ISBN-13: 978-1-6322-1263-4
eBook ISBN-13: 978-1-6322-1264-1

One four-line stanza from the Eagles song "Take it to the Limit" is used for illustration purposes only.

Memento Lapsos Bellator: *Remember the Fallen Warrior*

www.kevinhorganbooks.com
www.corps2corporate.com
www.ourcultureinchoate.com
https://anchor.fm/kevin-horgan

To my wife, Maureen

1

O ctober was the worst month of my life and Billy was at the center of it all.

Billy Bowman has always been my oldest friend. We served and trained together in Officer Candidate School (OCS), which is like an officer boot camp, and The Basic School (TBS), which is unique to the Marine Corps in that all officers get the same military training in weapons, land navigation, history, command structure, you name it. And pushups, lots of pushups.

I tell people Billy and I grew up together, which is a stretch. He went to Infantry Officer Class, an intense infantry leadership regimen, and I went to Supply School. We were to receive disparate orders and did not connect again until I was out of the Corps four years later and he was about to be separated. We joked that they needed to keep us apart, that the good name and integrity of the USMC officer corps was at risk any time after midnight if we were in the same bar.

Billy is taller than me by almost half a head although it looks like two feet. Even now, both of us in our 50's, he is crazy fit, lean, and muscled like cable. I've gotten quite soft, which I keep telling myself is only temporary.

After the first Gulf conflict we both got out of the Corps for strangely similar reasons, without comparing notes. We'd had enough. Loved it, hated it, tired of it. Career service in the military, lifelong service, is truly a calling. It didn't call me, and I suspect it didn't call Billy. But the foundation was laid, and we built lives from it, linked by temperament.

OCTOBER 1

From the street a single light shone from the hallway of my corner house, the same one I kept on all day and all night, a side window facing the neighbor and my driveway. It cast a beacon into the street and illuminated most of the curtained first floor. Pulling into the driveway at about ten at night, another average work and play schedule for me, I was reassured that all was as it should be. I was safe, again. I killed the ignition, cracked the car door open, and heard a laugh and breaking glass.

I kept a single stack 9mm in the vehicle. I had to think twice of where it was, and again of whether I had chambered a round. Fumbling in the console, I gripped the pistol and scrambled out of the car, crouched low, heart thundering.

Silence. I stayed low and assumed what passed for a tactical stance with my paunch in the way. My heart hammered in fear, and my head throbbed in time with it. I crept forward, one step, stop, listen. Again. My legs were on fire and my night vision was hampered by the glow at my head, to the left, of the hallway light. I heard a scruff in front of me by the patio. I racked the gun and it sounded too loud in the night quiet.

A high-pitched curse, a shout, and the runners were off the brick patio into my yard. I followed without purpose, relieved the burglars took flight. Two kids, or very small fast men, jumped the back split rail fence and charged into the dense woods behind the block. Impossible to track at night, and even in my boozy state I knew it was stupid and dangerous to chase anyone with a loaded gun.

My breathing was raspy and loud as I surveyed my patio and back door. The kids had broken the pedestrian door window. As I walked closer to inspect, I heard a familiar voice behind me.

"Clem." Flat, simple, controlled.

I wheeled, arms outstretched down, pistol pointed away. Instinct telegraphed a friendly.

"You okay, man?" Game Jackson was my neighbor, as steady a customer as I have ever known. Big dude, he did twenty years in the army. He had a cigar on his raised porch almost every evening but tonight I couldn't smell the Cohiba. I believe he and I were the loneliest men in town.

He had his twelve gauge at port arms.

Exhaling as if puking, I barked a laugh.

"Yeah, Game, I'm fine. I'm fine. Did you see 'em?"

"Heard 'em. Didn't see 'em 'til they hit the woods. Teenagers, maybe younger. Yeah, heard the glass and went for this," he held up the Mossberg, "and came out and saw you first."

"Yeesh. I didn't know what to think."

"Reeger, if you have to rack a pistol you leave in your car you won't need it, unless you plan to club someone with it. It misses the point."

My head was still a little foggy, and I shook it hard. He was probably right.

Game stayed with me as I swept up the glass and he helped me with cardboard to secure the opening until I could get a repairman to the house. He told me I could replace the glass cheap enough myself if I chatted up the Home Depot guy, but I just grunted dismissively. We both decided it was best to not call the police. It was after midnight when he said good-night, asking me for the tenth time if I was okay.

"I'm fine, Game. For the tenth time."

"You still seem a little tight, Clem. Get some sleep."

"Yeah. Yeah. Good night."

2

OCTOBER 2

I was up before six, chugged a big can of V8, chased that with Alka-Seltzer, my proven home remedy. Although still dark outside, I was wide awake, so I made a 12-cup pot of coffee rather than go pod-for-pod with the Keurig. No work until 10 am.

I paced up and down the hallway nursing my first cup, looking at the furniture, knick-knacks and photos collected in a 20-year relationship with Judith. Our un-marriage. Much of it was heavy, ornate and both gaudy and eclectic. We bought everything in this house together, agreeing on most of it, discussing placement and accents. We were proud of the house, the contents, the neighborhood and neighbors, and having the money to afford it. Now all I noticed was the visible cobweb where we used to sit together in front of the fireplace.

We've been separated for over a year. The place seemed empty and hollow, and now I noticed how crowded and complicated the rooms were. I could appreciate it, but I didn't like it. Without Judith it was suffocating. It was hard to say if my head hurt from a hangover or emotional overload, but I needed air.

I walked out the back door, inspecting my repair work. Not bad; I would call my administrative assistant, Luette, to get someone here to fix it, despite what Game suggested. Eyeing the back patio, I saw a muddy footprint that was out of place. I stood next to it and my size nine dwarfed the caked mud of the interloper. Definitely a kid. I might have shot him. Or her.

Game was up, standing on his deck. He waved, smiled, and gave me a thumbs up. I saluted in return, grateful for his presence, and he turned and went inside his well-lit kitchen, pausing only to glance at my car for an exaggerated second or three. I followed his line of sight at a leisurely pace.

Both right side tires of my Audi were off the driveway and firmly on the lawn. Not by a little, either. A ribbon of mud and crushed grass extended to the sidewalk fifty feet away. I walked most of its length, and as the sun began to rise, I took the steps up to my front porch, sat, and leaned back to the square pillar that held our flag. Only my flag, now. The porch was the best part of the house and the envy of all who walked or drove by it. I had not spent an evening on it since Judith moved out. But mornings were different.

I enjoyed the dawn, the routine sounds and smells and the promise of a fresh start. I closed my eyes and let the gentle warmth of the rising sun touch my face.

A bark and a thud. I might have been sleeping for a second or an hour, but the light had not improved appreciably. The morning paper was at the bottom of the stairs and the delivery guy who threw it there from his car probably did not notice me. As I uncoiled myself and went to retrieve the paper a nice-looking neighbor-lady I had named Mrs. Yoga Pants was walking her nice-looking dog, a large black creature with a white face and piercing black eyes She walked at a hearty pace and waved dutifully with her blue bag hand as the other strained against the frenetic prancing dog.

I enjoy reading the morning paper almost as much as I enjoy looking at Mrs. Yoga Pants.

The light was getting better by the second, and I could easily make out the headlines and bylines as the front page burst into full view. A banner article under the fold near the bottom read: "22 Veteran Suicides A Day, Unchanged From Ten Years Ago." Underneath that was a short squib on "*Heroes Who Hike on High,*" a web address, and a local phone number.

I thought it a strange name, the ad or article must have cost a pretty penny, or the publisher committed to run it gratis, but space didn't allow it until today. This was not a marijuana legal state, and the paper was top class, a real buttoned-down outfit of conservative opinion. A little too much for Judith and me, but reliable in news, articles, and ads.

Judith loved the ads. In the year or so since she walked out, I think of her intensely when I grip the pullouts, and that first month I saved them for her. Now I toss them out in self-disgust.

I walked back inside at not quite six-thirty. Sitting at the kitchen table I made a hasty list of to-do items, most for Luette, a couple for me. Quick work. I chugged another V8 and started to feel human with a semblance of energy on my third cup of coffee.

I put Billy's name at the top of my list. He hit the gym every day at 0600 no matter what time he crawled in the night before. Billy was a machine, a model of good care and conditioning. He called himself his own billboard. He was a teacher at the high school and taught Algebra I and II, and he was known as "Coach B." But every man has his vices, and we shared one in particular. Bourbon.

Billy coached freshman wrestling and baseball and scouted for varsity football. Coach B was a beloved fixture to both students and faculty and was especially popular with parents. He lived for being physical and set as good an example as possible for the kids, and not a few dads, too. He was loud and rowdy and worked to remember every kid's name and his bald pate, chiseled physique, and square jaw gave him a Mr. Clean appearance that was often remarked on.

He had a quality I never mastered. He never used profanity, publicly or privately. Coach B reasoned that setting an example was paramount for adults in a high school setting, especially coaches. Billy never hesitated to correct any coach, teacher, or parent if a vulgarity came forth, and everyone knew it and complied, which was sometimes real tough duty.

I checked my voicemail and listened without listening, one from Luette, and one from Marco Flocario, my oldest and biggest customer and sometime ally. I hung up and decided to go on offense and dump my laundry list of to-dos and do-whats on my AA, first, to include someone to repair my backdoor window and get the dope on *Heroes Who Hike on High*, or *HHH*.

Then I turned my attention to Marco's message, and since there was only one I assumed it was routine. When he was flustered, I could count on half a dozen voicemails in one evening. I listened a second time.

It was a long voicemail. He screamed, he threatened, he was abusive. Marco accused me of avoiding him (true), of professional duplicity (not sure what that was), of incompetence (meh), of my company's numerous failures with his product modifications including an annual roll-out that went flat (mostly true), of me being useless to my employer (ridiculous), of being a drunk (he should talk, the fat bastard), and being worthless as a man and unworthy of being a former officer of Marines.

The fact that he was mostly right on all counts didn't make me appreciate his insight or vitriol. I hated the guy most of the time, and if he wasn't my company's biggest customer and my sole direct customer account I would have throttled him years ago even though I was half his size.

But I wouldn't or couldn't. I am a coward. Judith would tell me I was not, that I had an obligation to the company and to her and even to Marco himself. I knew better.

I popped a cola, chugged half, thinking a burp midstream in my brief voicemail back to Marco would be appropriate. Marco would be shocked by a voice message from me before 0700.

I pushed the numbers carefully to get his private box.

"MOFO, you done? Good. I have a ten o'clock, but I can hustle that and meet you for an early dinner. How's four pm, at the Tap Room? I'll be there either way."

I knew MOFO would get him. Like Billy and me, Marco attended OCS and TBS at the same time. He became a CH-46 pilot and was given the call sign MOFO. Assigning call signs is not akin to Top Gun movie fame. You get a name that is embarrassing or indicative of a single or series of screw-ups. MOFO was an easy fit, alliterative of his name. Marco pretended he hated MOFO, apologizing to non-veterans all the time, but I knew he loved it.

Marco had been in country in Saudi Arabia for two weeks when he bounced a CH-46 too hard and ten Marines, including himself and the co-pilot, got whiplash, broken teeth, and serious back problems. The Sea Knight was down for a month. MOFO spent the rest of Desert Shield as a scheduler in a neck brace. He carried a huge chip on his shoulder as a result, and was forever brutal on anyone in his line of sight in the accountability department.

I hung up the phone, holding the burp I intended to punctuate the dinner and drinking invite. After that tirade of his I had to stay professional until he went soft on me, which he always did, but not until he had a couple drinks in him.

I lived and worked an hour east of the City, and Marco lived an hour west of it. We met, at least once a month, in City Center for dinner and drinks and sometimes trouble, but as the years pulled us downhill we mostly sat around and told lies. Which is why Billy was so important to get in the loop for tonight.

Marco loved Billy. Man to man, martial arts, guns, and tribal stories about being born on the wrong side of the tracks and a misspent youth. When I needed to smooth out Marco, I invited Billy, who loved Marco right back, at least most of the time.

I had to talk to Billy, right away. If I had showed up at the gym at 0600 he would have dropped dead from shock, but I calculated that I could meet him as he was leaving to head to school. His routine was rigid. Billy left the gym at 0710 and arrived at the school flagpole by 0720 to bark, cajole and say hey to every kid, and it seemed he knew them all, girl or boy, by name or nickname.

I skipped the shower and shave and put on my best casual ensemble. Trousers were too tight, but I could fix that tomorrow.

At 0709 I drove into the gym's parking lot and almost hit Billy's ten-year-old Chevy. He jumped from the car, annoyed but grinning.

"Hey, Stupid! You were going to call last night when you got home! What happened, you okay?"

I forgot he wanted to talk to me, and I was not then in any condition for something heavy, anyway. He would have been over to my place in half a second with bloodhounds and tracked those kids until dawn if necessary. I waved my hands.

I got out of my car. "Yeah, yeah, all good. Sorry, I, uh, had too much to drink and just crapped out. All good."

Billy shrugged, the smile easing away.

"Yeah, we can talk later if you can manage it." He was a little ticked off, uncharacteristic of him.

"Come with me to the Tap Room tonight, Billy. Marco and I are doing an early dinner."

I thought he'd bite right away. Marco's name raised his eyebrows, and early dinner, code for tying one on, brought that Billy smile, but just for a moment. He shrugged, again.

"Man, I can't. There's a craft fair I promised the club I'd be at...freshman girls, don't want to disappoint them."

"A commitment? Or just a see-you-there?" I grinned idiotically.

His conflict and conviction were evaporating like dew at dawn. The Tap Room on Thursday night was a terrific place to start the weekend. I told him I had reservations at 1600.

He caved. "Okay, Clem, you drive. I can be free at two-forty-five. Meet me here, you know the drill. Now get out of my way." Billy was smiling again.

I sat back in my car and backed up enough for him to pass, then pulled into his spot. Stabbing the phone, I left a message for Luette to make reservations for tonight. Billy usually had me meet him at the gym if I was driving. He had a full locker and first-class privileges there, teaching classes and subbing for trainers in case of absenteeism. They paid him cash, and Billy didn't schedule anything that wasn't convenient. He was the gym's fireman, a fill-in for any absent trainer, and it worked out great for all parties. "My second home," he called it.

I went home for a nap.

@@@@@

Early for the 1000, I sat alone in the conference room we used for all meetings, from birthdays to announcements to client sales to staff reviews to hiring and firing. Today's meeting was a routine scheduled staff affair of the nine decision makers, and I came to it prepared, as usual, with big stories and little data. I jiggled my Rolex for the umpteenth time that morning. I loved my watches.

I have a healthy disdain for these monthly half-day events and had my ready excuse for ditching at mid-afternoon – a meeting with our biggest client, Marco Flocario of Flocario Enterprises. Everyone would shut up after that. Marco paid the light bills, and much of the salaries. I did have a couple important issues to review with Production and R&D, whose department heads were decent and hard-working managers.

Which means they despised me. I avoided public confrontation with them. Even though they had to comply with Marco's complicated issues, they tended to complain loudly, and since I was the messenger, they took it out on me. With customers and peers I absorbed a lot of abuse in the name of collegiality, even if it was a one-way street.

Our company's product is a compilation of several unique patented items made off-shore, shipped in bulk here, and then cobbled together in our only factory to make our simple generic and protected product, which we modify on demand, accounting for much of our profit. Every home has a couple of these units, though only your plumber or electrician knows it. If you are a fix-it guy you've broken or replaced these things over the years. But you would also be careful; they are not cheap. Easily modified for local use, we license the primary product to some, make adjustments for others, and completely alter the specs and use (retaining proprietary rights) for still others. The industry calls it the "T-Cup."

I have worked for my company since I left the service over 20 years ago, except for a brief hiatus biking to Mexico. I say brief, because after two weeks of cycling through the Southwest I had my bike stolen within 30 minutes of being in Mexico. I gave a kid five dollars to watch it outside a bodega while I used the head. When I came out, the bike and the kid were gone. Billy never let me forget that, either.

And I am a co-founder, owning a large but not majority share of several of the patents and a boatload of private shares. I opted to stay with the firm because I like being a part of it, though I could have cashed out long ago, very comfortably. A small whisper of guilt keeps me from just taking my cut and walking away.

I know how we inbound the different product, store it, build the generic T-Cup, fulfill orders, send random product to R&D, provide intellectual property security, use our own tool and die department to feed production of specials, transport material through numerous carriers, advertise through trade publications, and sift through potential high value revenue customers. The pieces are made overseas, but we modify and assemble the T-Cup here in one state of the art location, east of the City.

Made in 'Murica, man. I jiggled my Rolex for the mega-umpteenth time.

I respect our management team. There's a ton of cash flow, but the people come first. The head honcho makes a great salary, but not an eye-popping one. There's real vision within the top brass of us nine, always looking at a variety of applications for maintaining long-reaching viability. We're frugal but not cheap. The front-line manufacturing operation is a very physical union-free environment, and those folks are committed to the company's success through a most satisfactory profit-sharing stock award paid out quarterly. If we didn't pay it out, they'd probably eat us.

As one of the longest tenured employees, and not exactly young, I enjoy picking and choosing my duties. I work the floor a couple times a week shaking hands and slapping backs, and I consider these people to be my friends, or at least very friendly.

Of the nine decision makers, the "committee," only four of us had ever worked the floor. I don't have to play that card, but they know it's in my hand. My peers, who work like donkeys, both tolerate and back bench me through their silence, though. Technically, I report to the Sales Department manager, but my substantial company holdings and patents allow me to ignore her, Wharton degree and all. I am the only military veteran on the staff.

The lights come on in the conference room. I had not realized I was sitting in near darkness.

The CEO and the HR department manager ambled in, gently closing the door behind them, taking seats near me and not near their normal positions at the head of the table. Slowly suspicious, I choked out a good morning, twitching the Rolex.

"Clem, we need to talk..."

@@@@@

I was parked in front of the gym well before Billy's arrival, stewing. There was no staff meeting. If I could have spoken to Judith, I think I would have calmed down sooner.

Billy pulled into the parking lot before three, grabbed a sport coat from his back seat, and bounced to my car. His grin lightened my mood even as the rain started to fall. He threw himself into the passenger seat.

"Man, I need this. I love those kids, Clem, I really do, but I am looking forward to eating, drinking, telling lies and howling at the moon..."

Putting the car in gear, I snorted through my nose. I knew he wasn't finished.

"...and maybe get lucky; how long has it been for you, twenty years?"

I tried to laugh but groaned instead.

"Wait, wait, you mean you're giving up your vow of chastity?" He clapped his face in mock surprise.

I laughed with sincerity and my black cloud started to lift.

We drove in silence for a few minutes, the rain becoming a torrent, and even in my custom car I needed to concentrate with both hands on the wheel, squinting and hunched over. Billy was casual about the rough weather, now blowing sideways, and he yawned, fiddling with the defroster. My vision improved immediately.

"Thanks." It came out dry.

"Dummy."

Ten more minutes of silence was an eternity for Billy.

"What's up your butt, Reeger? Rough half day at work?"

I envied Billy. Admired and envied. The local high school where he made a career wanted him and needed him. He was a fixture for the freshmen, as beleaguered a group as God ever created, and was very popular with parents. Coach B was a calming though kinetic influence for any student on his radar for all four years. Passionate about coaching ball teams, he attended as many school events as he could, always arriving in style and cheering like every minute was his last.

Billy served in the first Gulf War, which we now know as Operation Desert Shield/Desert Storm, as did Marco, as did I. He was also married and divorced during his four-year stint, and was never inclined to marry again, though he was frequently in the company of lovely women when the occasion allowed. Billy has a tattoo of the Crown of Thorns on his back-right shoulder blade, without color, which he got when he was a teen. He went to Catholic church weekly, though we never discussed it. Except for funerals, I haven't been in a church of my faith since my mother died decades ago.

Billy told a yarn better than anyone, ever, and if exaggeration and hyperbole requires a patron saint it would be Billy Bowman.

"Every day something hilarious happens, Clem. You just don't see it. And I remember all the funny stuff."

At the time I couldn't let it pass. "And you never let the facts get in the way, either, Coach."

"Goodness, no. Why would I do that?"

He read a ton, memorizing poems and challenging students and faculty alike to tussle with his prodigious if scattered memory. A devotee of Rudyard Kipling and Robert Service, he appreciated their fallen villains and redemptive heroes.

But Billy succumbed to dark fugues of his own, several times a year. Never lasting more than a day or two, during these times he would maintain his rigid schedule, yet suffered through a lack of connectivity with everyone except Judith and me. Some people would confuse it with being snobbish. Others would try to pry him open. I ignored him. On those occasions we would sit on my front porch, in silence, as he stared at the palms of his hands.

Just as randomly he would come out of it. "Hey, Clem, want to catch a movie?"

Billy didn't eat much, seeing food only as fuel. Other than books, his weaknesses were a good steak, Gentleman Jack or Evan Williams, and his damn bugle. He couldn't play anything except reveille, Taps, and a couple popular blasts, and kept it in a hard briefcase, often at the ready. Among his many annoying and predictable uses for it, he played "Charge!" before Chess Club matches, making even those kids cool.

And he was ready to let loose tonight, but all I wanted was to feel sorry for myself, and pout to my ex-girlfriend.

"So, what's really eating you, Reeger? We've got an hour and you can't run away."

"Billy…" I choked, and it came out like a sob.

"Dude. Spit it out. What. Happened."

I started with the kids attempting the break in, the gun, where I drove my car, Game helping me, the dawn, the newspaper, Marco's voicemail, and then I paused.

"Sounds like a routine day in the life of Clem Reeger, to me. You want to dry out or something? Marco giving you the creeps?"

"Yeah. Maybe. No, man, that's not it. I met with the CEO and head of HR today. They want me out. It was an ambush. They're asking right now, but I know they don't have to ask!" I sighed.

"Crap. What did they say?" Billy's concern was genuine. He rolled his head and neck and let out a yap.

"The boss started first. Gave me fluff about my tenure, my value as a legacy employee, but he finished his speech with 'you are not invaluable.' Then the HR person started in."

"You trust her?" I felt him looking into my ear.

"Yeah, she's okay, great, actually. She came up from the floor like me and the boss and the Operations guy. We're the last legacy people of the nine on the committee."

"Does she trust you?"

I rolled my head, listening to the snaps in my neck competing with the fast thump of the wipers.

Before the ubiquity of the internet and GPS, we all needed to write down directions, make plans, and develop contingencies. Memorize stuff. We lived to be disappointed by small details and we didn't know it. My greatest disappointment was myself. Why would anyone trust me?

During the most intense periods of the storm, as the traffic naturally slowed, we made off-hand comments. We avoided asking each other questions. He yawned and yapped frequently, either because he was tired or he could be going into one of his fugues, a day or so of uncommunicative behavior. I would have welcomed it now, but I needed a third leg of the stool dealing with Marco tonight. I extended my fingers as if ready to grip the storm ahead of me, and squeezed the steering wheel, hard.

"Have you spoken to Judith?"

I shook my head.

"Lay it out for her. She has good instincts." He nodded as I glanced at him.

I thought about calling Judith right there and then, but I resisted the impulse because it necessitated privacy.

"Hey, Slim. Now is a perfect time to call Judith," Billy said gently.

That snapped me out of my reverie. The rain still came in gusts and bursts, but instinct kept me driving competently and unconsciously.

"I can get rid of these pounds in a week or two, no problem." I wanted to change the subject, away from Judith.

"That's laughable, Clem. We aren't kids anymore. You have twenty extra pounds, maybe more, and you sure as heck don't take care of yourself." I could feel him shaking his head and grinning.

Judith is only a few inches shorter than my slouching 5'9". Always thin, her blond hair is full and shoulder length kept in a perpetual ponytail. Her eyes are huge, blue and expressive, and her smile would melt a glacier. Judith is beautiful, feminine, intense, fun and funny. Just thinking about her brought me a knowing smile of my own and a gut punch of regret.

"I want to lose some weight before I, you know, call her," I mumbled.

"That's nice. Total crap, man, but nice. She doesn't care about that. But she does care that you don't care."

I didn't need this while fighting both the storm and developing traffic. "Save it, Billy. Now's not the time."

@@@@@

The Tap Room in the City was our go-to place, the singular thing the three of us agreed on, joking that it was our neutral site. The place was all wood and beveled glass, on the dark side, with a friendly and accommodating wait staff, great food and generous drinks. Pricey, but we didn't care. I regularly picked up the tab. Even Judith liked the place, back in the day. I never had a problem getting a good table as I spent a small fortune of the company's money there. On busy nights they added tables to accommodate reservations. I always asked for and received a curved booth deep in the main dining room.

It was crowded already at 1600, even on Thursdays.

Marco was waiting for us, halfway through (apparently) his first cocktail. He was unfailingly punctual and seethed when I was less than ten minutes early, like today.

"I don't know why I put up with you." He shook his massive head and jet-black mane with it. Billy was convinced he dyed it.

I was still smarting from the meeting today, and the drive in the teeming rain didn't help. I had unloaded everything about my general failures to Billy, who a-hemmed and uh-huh-ed at all the right times. If I strayed into whining territory, or tried to cast blame elsewhere, Billy pounced.

"Knock it off," Coach B would say on many an occasion.

I owned it, all of it. A failed relationship. A fall at the height of a career based on a lucky discovery and the pursuit of ease. My last contribution of real value to anything and anyone was my uninspired military service, a generation ago, in a war that had to be re-fought. Billy, Marco, and I shared many things: esprit de corps without distinction, an appreciation for booze and impulsive behavior, and the exact same birthday: April 21, 1968, a date sandwiched in between the assassinations of King and Kennedy during the summer of love.

The three of us served as USMC officers during the late 80's. It's a small club, we knew the same commanders and staff NCO's, and we tend to have the same habits, predictable and boring to everyone except ourselves. Billy was supremely athletic, and led by jockstrap, which was typical, and approved by leadership, peers and subordinates back in the day. Marco made it through helicopter flight training and was wonkish, well-read in technical manuals and knew the nomenclature of not just the entire US arsenal, but the then-Soviet and Chinese as well. His command of these weapon systems was thorough and impressive, if not outright numbing, but respected by the officer class. He really dug it and it showed.

Billy, Marco, and I ran around together while stationed in Quantico, back in the day.

Both Billy and Marco were consummate young professional officers back then. I was somewhere in between them both physically and academically and did not have a yearning to excel as much as a drive to prove something to myself, that I could cut it. If my peers did not know it, I did: I was a young leader of Marines for unpatriotic reasons. I left the Corps after my initial commitment and never looked back. Billy and Marco both left, too, Billy reluctantly and Marco kicking and screaming. I never pressed them for the "why" and the only time any of us thought back out loud it was all "Oorah" and Semper fi.

I was still in a fog as I slid to one side of Marco, and Billy the other. The booth was perfect for the three of us, or two couples. Marco glowered at me and Billy looked distracted and elsewhere.

"Hello, MOFO, you look like you've been here all day," I said, trying to ease the heavy pall over the table.

The waitress, who looked like her day was going poorly, approached, forced a thin smile, and nodded at Billy.

"Two of whatever our dad is having." He flashed his best smile and got a big one in return.

Marco snickered and for a second his scowl vanished. Marco loved all of Billy's tired jokes and imitated them whenever he could get the jump on either of us. His foul humor today had him off his usual bonhomie.

"Wet out there, Marco. Doesn't look like you were caught in it," said Billy, an eyebrow cast at Marco in either recrimination or jest.

Marco snorted and swigged his drink. Then silence, and the waitress returned quickly.

"Yeah, been here a while." He downed the rest of it. "I'll have another, please, and make sure this guy," he thumbed in my direction, twice, "gets the check."

"Dinner, boys?" She was warming to us and looked like she would rather sit with us than be on her feet. Since I was paying for this night, I took some semblance of control.

"Yes, we will, but no menus yet. How 'bout some pretzels and nuts, the usual munchies?" I smiled.

She gave a knowing nod and was off in a hurry. We stared at her walking away. They both turned to me.

I bristled. "What, you guys don't like pretzels, now?"

Marco cut me off. "You're both soaked. Should have asked her for a towel."

The drinks came with pretzels and mixed nuts, two big bowls, and we chewed and crunched and slugged our whiskey on the rocks in silence. I was waiting for Billy to start in with a tall tale, but he was just reading Marco, who looked at his own wrists as if he didn't know how to operate them. Marco had huge forearms, bigger than mine by plenty but not as defined as Billy's. Their size alone screamed "don't screw with me" and could not be hidden by the tailor-made French cuffs of his shirt. Marco made a fist.

"Clem, listen. I was going to blister you after dinner. I can't wait. We have a problem." His gaze moved to my face and he held it just above my chin. Marco was struggling.

I finished my drink and waved it as the waitress passed. She eyed the table and nodded.

Marco cleared his throat. "I know they lowered the boom on you today. You deserved it, man. You just don't know why."

"Sure, I do. I had a, well, generally bad year." I squinted.

"What? Generally bad? Are you kidding?" He leaned closer to me. "You've always been generally bad, but tolerable. This last year was almost criminally irresponsible!"

Billy shot a hand out. "Whoa, Marco, don't..."

"Stay out of it, Coach." Marco leaned back. "Look, Clem, your board doesn't care for me, and I generally don't respect them. You're just the middle guy. But you need to do something, anything, sometime. All you do is eat and drink on an expense account.'

I tried sounding tough. "Wait a minute..."

"No, you wait. We've known each other too long to mince words."

The waitress arrived with menus and fresh drinks. Billy tried to lighten all of it. "What's your name, young lady?"

She didn't answer right way, and probably sensed a long night nursing us along. "Gwen." I looked at her in gratitude. She smiled at me in pity, saying she'd be back in a few. We said thanks all around.

Marco almost hissed at me, "For a year I've been asking for better competitive reports."

"Hey, man, it's been rough for him, Judith and all." Billy's voice was steady and low which came out as a growl.

"Yeah, I know. Been there, boys. Best medicine is work. Throw yourself into it. I honestly don't know what the heck you've been doing, Reeger."

"I'm on the job, Marco," I squeaked, pitched too high.

"You ain't working, or working out, either. You look terrible, your face is drawn, and your eyes are always puffy. You don't communicate with your board or committee or whatever and you sure as heck don't respond to what I've been telling you for nearly a year!" He was working himself into a spitting mess as I tried to shrink into my seat.

Billy drained his drink and waved it for another, effectively giving up my defense. I ground my teeth at my own inadequacies. Marco was right and I was going to slow down starting tonight. Billy was going to keep pace with Marco, likely thinking that racing Marco to goofiness would take some pressure off me.

"Marco, I have heard your requests, every word of them." I sat up straighter.

"What? You've heard, Marine? You heard? But you didn't listen, Clem."

I could only try to stutter. I was praying he wouldn't ask me to recite his requests. I would not be able to give him one concrete specific.

"For a year I've been talking product, asking for a competitive analysis..."

I had to defend myself. "But you have people doing that!"

Marco turned to Billy. "You see?"

Billy stared at the mirror over my head, distracted. "See what?"

Marco' exasperation became resignation. "How about just listening now?" He paused, biting his lip. "I wanted your company to take on my competitors. I wanted your vision on how I could increase market share. I wanted your personal partnership of my business, a fresh look. My people are good, damn good, but they aren't perfect, they tend to look inside." He cracked his knuckles.

I would not interrupt. Marco filled the void. "I had a plan and you didn't tell your board."

I had no idea what he was talking about.

"You have no clue, do you? Two years ago you could finish my sentences." He looked sad.

"I, I'm sorry." I was sorry for myself and not his lofty ideas.

Marco slammed his hand on the table. "Stop that! I wanted you to approach your board about me buying out the line. I've been hinting at it for over a year. Let me manufacture my own T-Cup. Gonna do it offshore, too. Lots cheaper."

I started my own slow swoon, stifling a yawn, and caught Billy's eye; his glance warned danger.

Marco charged ahead. "And now it's too late, for you. My lawyers say I don't have to buy it. It's mine, through some goofy legal karate. It's mine. That's a whole lotta revenue you guys are out."

I was stunned, too overwhelmed to speak. This could crater my company.

Marco charged ahead. "I called your boss last night, your CEO. I guess he checked with his attorneys, and the whole mess would be too costly to litigate for him..."

I started to breathe again.

"And he, Reeger, he's a smart cookie, he suggested a merger. Mostly my terms, he keeps other T-Cup production here. That means a big scale-off of people, but..."

I stopped breathing.

"... At least the company is afloat."

I hiccupped. "Oh, Lord, what have I done?"

"It's not what you did, Clem. It's what you failed to do. Omission. A grave corporate sin. That Bronze Star doesn't count for much now, huh?"

Billy and I both cut him off. Marco always steamed about that, something I never had control over, something I knew I didn't deserve. I would not go down that road tonight.

The waitress drifted by. Billy took charge. "Gwen, three petit filets, medium rare, and a big bowl of mashed potatoes and creamed spinach, please. Another round, too."

"Not for me." I covered my glass. She glided away.

Marco leaned over to me. "Clem, we may take the merged company public. Inside shareowners of both companies will win big time. At least a 100% gain overnight.

Despite myself, I smiled broadly. I was now wealthy, but this had crazy potential. "Not too bitter a pill, Marco. Genius."

Billy woke up. "What about the average guy on the floor?"

Marco coughed. "They'll make a few bucks, too, if they held shares. Not enough to retire on, probably. Most will find new jobs, somewhere."

My smile vanished. "Oh, no." My friends on the floor would hate me forever, and I didn't have a lot of friends.

Marco laid his paw on my forearm. "One other thing, Clem. My last condition. You're out. That's why they initiated the talk with you today. Seems like either way, you're out."

@@@@@

Marco rambled through dinner, alternating between sports, his ex-wife, his new wife, two ungrateful children in college, politics, and pounding my skull for good measure. I parried as much as I reasonably could, but it didn't matter that Billy and I were even there. Marco could eat like a horse and talk lucidly with much of his mouth full while half drunk.

Billy rose at one point. "Got to hit the head. Hey, Slim, here's five dollars. Watch my drink." He set the folded five-spot under my plate and started for the men's room.

Marco roared, scaring patrons close by. "I knew you'd get to that, Billy! I knew it!"

I hated the gag as much as I hated being called Slim. I chuckled on cue and pocketed the fin.

The waitress and a busboy cleared our plates. Gwen brought Billy and Marco another round. I had switched to club soda; I had to drive.

Marco stretched. "Last one for me, boys. I guess it'll be a while before we get together. Hey, we're still friends, right?"

Marco's little speech must have been for Billy, because a nearly thirty year friendship with me was over. We were never really friends. It's not that Marco didn't like me; it is that I knew he no longer respected me, and perhaps he never did. Marco was holding out to remain on good terms with Billy.

Billy stared at him, in the hard fashion that he reserved for recalcitrant testosterone fueled teenagers, or referees who were lazy, or people who were just plain sloppy. Billy pounced.

"No, Marco, we're not friends." His voice was thick, whether emotion or the whiskey.

Marco blustered. "This is business..." He poked a thumb in my direction.

"Bull. You're a thug. Know this, MOFO, you strip a man of his dignity and he's worthless to you. So are his friends. Clem is my brother. You think I will let this slide so we can drink together and chase strippers? You nuts? Go ahead and finish your drink. Alone."

I was already up and out of my seat when Billy said "brother." I waved to the waitress to meet me at the bar and I paid the bill. Billy walked straight out and didn't look back.

@@@@@

We spent the first five minutes on the drive home in silence. It had stopped raining.

Billy spoke first. "I think I hate that guy."

"I do now," I sneered, "but he's right."

"Doesn't matter. He's coarse and cheap and blames you for failing to communicate." Billy's "communicate" came out "communa-cake."

I wanted to set Billy straight. "You didn't need to say anything."

"I know, Clem. Not about you. He's a bum. Had it coming."

"Thanks, anyway."

"Clem, can you give me one reason to talk to that ass ever again?"

"No," I answered quickly. Billy didn't use foul language and this breach was not lost on me.

He wheezed. "Then I won't. Screw him, right?" Billy stretched, lightly hitting his head on the car door window glass. We both laughed at the absurdity of it all. He was hammered. I could sense him looking at me as I struggled to focus on the road.

We didn't speak again until we got out of the city proper and made the highway home.

"Billy, I think about that medal a lot, how I didn't deserve or want it."

"Reeger, I think about those kids every day." He slept as the rain drummed hard. When I dropped him off forty minutes later we didn't even say good night.

3

OCTOBER 3

The next morning I rolled out of bed unrefreshed, needing more sleep, but with a clear head.

I called Judith at 0700. She was always an early riser. I asked her if she'd like to go to dinner and was met with silence.

"You there, Judith?"

"Yes." Very quiet, almost a whisper. Then a sigh. "No, not dinner."

I stifled a gasp, but it came out like a sob.

"Oh, God, Clem, what's wrong?" Still whispering.

"Nothing, nothing. I thought I was going to sneeze, and it came out wrong." I faked a laugh.

Judith snickered, and sighed again, only this time with a happy ring. "I thought you had ulterior motives, then I thought you were in some sort of crisis."

"Ulterior..." I was genuinely surprised.

"Oh, never mind, Clem. Dinner is out."

I hid my disappointment but pushed on. "I want to discuss some personal matters with you."

I could hear her intake of breath. "Uh, yes?"

"I lost my job." I tried to sound clinical and unemotional. If I was out of work, the money spigot would taper off at some point, and might put a small cramp in her lifestyle and ambition.

Silence. Then she roared in laughter, real guffaws, which I had not heard from her in years.

"What took them so long?"

We both laughed now, hard, and she was crying, I know she was, because when she experienced the ironic or beautiful or awful, she could find something funny in it. I loved her desperately, and the tightness in my chest and throat kept me from telling her, again, just to get another chuckle.

Judith settled down and tried to apologize. Cutting her off, I stumbled through "sorries" and for not asking about her and her work, first, by way of greeting.

"Thank you, Clem." She sounded bright and lovely, but the emotions bubbled and she kept sniffling through the call. "Tell me, please."

It took me the better part of an hour, but I laid it all out, what happened. I deflected blame. She sniffled. I accepted responsibility. She blew her nose. I hinted at an interest in *HHH*, and she thought that was splendid.

I was spent, and paused to inventory my thoughts and emotions.

"Do you have a cold, Judith?"

"No. I have a dog."

She wasn't emotional; she was allergic or close to it. My presumptions are notoriously wrong.

Judith always wanted a dog, grew up with them, and I threw a cold blanket on that early in our relationship. Begging that I was deathly allergic, I said no way, even faking an itchy rash or sneeze attack in the enclosed presence of anything furry. It was all a lie. I simply did not want my life to revolve around any animal other than me.

"Oh, uh, what kind?"

She tried to giggle but hacked on phlegm. "Bassett Hound. Kind of a mix, but I think the daddy was a really, really slow Bassett Hound."

"What's its name?" I suspected she could see me shaking my head over the phone.

"Baby-face. And I'm allergic to him." She sighed, and I struggled to say something glib.

"But I have to keep him. Let me blow my nose and put him outside."

"Okay, but would you rather I call later?"

"No," she whispered, "Wait for me."

I waited for her to come back on the line. After ten minutes, I hung up, tried calling back, and it went to voicemail. I considered getting in the car and driving over to her place, but the last time I did so she told me never to do that again, unless invited. For the life of me I did not know what drove her away.

@@@@@

Judith has great instincts, and she's famous, too, in a local, albeit narrow, sense. My lady the artist has a unique form of expression, which is bold, original, and something most people get used to even if they don't quite "get it." Judith takes tin and taps out an image using a variety of household items from a ballpeen hammer to a straight pin. Using her hands, she contours the pliant metal so it rolls gently under her hand onto a surface. Then she solders a small handle, applies paint, single or multi-colored, and rolls her tin-pan (her words) onto a surface, normally canvass, but she took to working on surfaces of wood, paper, and glass. Her use of paint is fascinating and distinctive.

Judith's art has been in demand in our town for street fairs and school projects. The younger school kids like banging the tin itself, which renders the tin-pan product vague and unrecognizable, while the older students see if they can make obscenities come to life when the reverse is rolled onto a surface. Given that young children with hammers, nails, and spiky tools need constant supervision, high school kids needed more.

And she loves it all. The art, the children, the combustibility of it all.

We never married, even after being exclusive for nearly twenty years. Her call. I begged her, I pleaded, I threatened... no dice, Judith would not budge. Hence, no children. My great sadness.

We talked around the issue. For the past several years I started apologizing for it, first with words and then with only a wan smile. Judith always stayed positive in my pain, perhaps in forgiveness or in melancholy, though always in union in our shared disappointment in each other's lack of commitment.

Judith has one near-masterpiece, and it hangs behind glass at our town hall. It's a pedestrian door, wood, without a knob, with a quarter inch upper and lower recess. The base color is a shiny white.

She started using a three-inch square tin-pan of a vague American face, to be used repeatedly on the surface. With much planning, trial and error and dozens of throw away tin pieces, the face took shape: hairless except eyebrows, soft eyes the outside of which sloped down imperceptibly, the nose small and flat, lips neither full or thin, but parted as if to begin speaking, chin with a gentle even cleft. Though clearly male, it could have been anyone and no one, though I always saw exaggerated features.

And each application changed the colors and contours and each face was unique.

If the face wasn't striking enough, Judith's tender usage was elegant and simple. On the glossy white surface she made the U.S. flag by rolling the tin-pan in appropriate and proportioned colors to simulate it, red, white, and blue. She made meticulous calculations, like a carpenter, that needed to be made to stay as close to the actual flag as possible without distortion. Billy volunteered the math for Judith and helped with fine-tuning the colors required sequentially on a drawn grid of the door.

From a distance of 100 feet it looks like a vertical hanging flag was painted on straight wood, and the opaque white on white of the stars and stripes give the flag the appearance of gently waving.

The blue field of white stars was the most time-consuming for her. Hand-painting the tin-pan with the colors to be transferred was unforgiving. No two stars are situated the same but are perfectly aligned and the face is clear throughout.

The white stripes posed a challenge, too. The face white-on-white was proving impossible to differentiate even using accents to note shadow. Judith used a pale eggshell and touches of grey which at first blush gave real depth to the face, without marring the white bars.

Remarkably, Judith used only the one tin-pan, and the painting, washing, pressure, and cosmic forces had some of the peaks of the face transfer deteriorate. It took three doors to get the effect right. Starting in the upper left corner, the blue field, she worked from left to right, measuring, painting, rolling, washing. Exceedingly time-consuming, the final effect was remarkable. The lower third of the door faded in clarity, the face gently receding, the color vivid but looking like torn cloth.

"The red stripes were easy," Judith told everyone who asked.

We showed it, at my insistence, almost ten years ago at a local gallery known for no serious traffic. *"A Face on the Flag"* was an instant hit, and after the first couple of days of people trying to touch the face(s), the gallery owner, who had the demeanor of a mortician and was not a showman, put up stanchions, placed it at the far end of the gallery, and the effect was perfect. As you entered the gallery you saw a painted down-facing flag, and as you walked toward it, the faces jumped out at you.

Offers to purchase it were made. Our favorite story was about the art critic from the City paper who came mid-day during the second week and looked at it for less than a minute, spoke to no one, and went to a tavern across the street. Writing nothing down, he ordered a beer and a sandwich, and made a one-hour phone call on his cell phone. He left his sandwich untouched, drained half the warm beer, and strode back toward the gallery. I matched his pace in the pedestrian dominated street – it was my job to keep an eye on him.

I approached him. "Everything okay?" I asked, with phony personal concern.

He smiled. "I saw you watching me. You know the artist?"

"Her boyfriend, name's Clem Reeger. We live together." He arched an eyebrow. "Really, for like ten years."

He did not offer his name but talked without breaking stride. He said he was on a mission, of sorts. I presumed he looked it over, bored, and had other pressing business to attend to. As we re-entered the gallery he went straight to the manager.

"I'm from the *Times*. Can you get these stanchions out of the way? Now?"

The manager clasped his hands, mumbled and started backing away. Igor the supplicant in the face of Dr. Frankenstein's genius.

"I'll assume that is a yes. Uh, the artist? You have contact information on her?" He ignored me completely.

Judith was sitting in another corner, surrounded by four pre-school children, and as the kids colored and played with stickers, she smiled and encouraged them, happy in their happiness, as the mothers gossiped and sipped Prosecco, and clucked at something disgusting that should not have been hung on another wall.

Igor pointed to Judith and then scurried out the front door. I knew the stanchions were too heavy for him, so I assumed he went to get help for moving them, something I started doing unbidden.

"That's Judith?" He asked no one. I nodded assent. He smiled broadly out of amusement, and offered his hand to me, introducing himself with one hand and snapping a business card toward me with the other.

"I'm *the* art critic for the *Times*. I think this piece is tremendous, tremendous. I phoned in most of my article already..."

My eyes went wide and my mouth popped open, and he laughed, gripping my upper arm.

"Really, buddy, I just want a few personal details to color in the story, so to speak. It will get in next Sunday's Arts Edition." He smiled.

My eyes welled, not a normal condition, and I mumbled, "Thanks."

"Could you ask her to give me a few minutes?"

At first I was indignant. "Why not ask her yourself? She doesn't need my help."

His chuckle was a little subdued, but genuine. "Of course not. But she may want to run a brush through her hair, go to the powder room. My photographer was supposed to be here 20 minutes ago. You know women, don't you?"

I nodded exaggeratedly and approached Judith, who appeared to have taken note of all the movements between the critic, Igor, and myself. She unfolded herself from playing on the floor with the children, winked at me, and before I could say a word, whispered, "I have to pee. Don't let him get away."

She had never looked so beautiful to me than that day. As she passed me, I whispered, "Photographer any minute now."

The piece ran two Sundays later, a color photo of the *Flag* taking up four columns and the top of the fold on page three of the *Times* Arts Section, with national circulation. By then Judith had received a bona fide offer of $20,000. She turned it down. The gallery kept it at eye level after that, stanchions 15 feet back for regular visitors, closer for collectors. Although Igor's floor space was shrinking, he was selling other pieces with the new foot traffic, even the disgusting ones.

Judith kept it at the gallery for a year until the Town Council asked to put it front and center in the Visitors' Center. She immediately agreed.

The only bad part of *A Face on the Flag* is that the original single tin-pan Judith used is gone. And there's only one door, but thousands of photo reproductions adorn everything from college dorms to PX's in Germany. The residual payments, "mailbox money" we called it, has been real nice but has predictably declined over the past couple years.

4

OCTOBER 4

The storefront was much like America, old and new, eclectic and mundane, washed out colors, broken concrete. The anchor store was a Hobby Lobby, always doing a brisk business. Moving east was a nail salon, a liquor store, a Christian artifact and book shop, a flooring emporium, a dry cleaner, and a ladies fabric and craft thing. The "V" of the plaza was crammed with recruiting stations for the Army, Navy, and Marine Corps. Business was always brisk there, too.

Cutting north were the five fast food joints: Chinese, pizza, subs, coffee and bagels, then a fried everything place. After Judith moved out, I have been a regular at all five for almost all my alone meals, and I am not proud of that. Next down the line was a deficient and too narrow store for anything but two desks, with a hand-painted banner: *Heroes Who Hike on High,* then the ubiquitous drugstore that did okay, but lacked a drive thru. It was an old outdoor shopping mall with 100% occupancy and was the quick stop center of our neighborhood.

I was excited and had momentum. Judith and Billy corroborated my need to do something important, maybe grand, and this might be it. I wore jeans and a sweatshirt and shaved even though it was Saturday. I was confident I could help these guys.

The *Heroes Who Hike on High* frontage was less than fifteen feet, glass with a single pedestrian door, internal blinds that were even, a message from the proprietor on military alignment. The glass had large "*HHH*" hand painted in red, with gold trim. Clean but worn.

Marching up to the door, I pulled where it said push. Annoyed at my error, I pushed, overdid it, and the glass shook when it hit the doorstop. My inertia kept me moving until I stood two feet from the first desk, which was unoccupied.

"Whoa, dude. How you makin' out?"

At the other desk, three feet back on the other side of the room, sat the scariest guy I have ever seen. Tattoos from the shoulders to mid forearms accented a bleached wife beater t-shirt straining against large flat muscles. Reddish brown Fu Manchu mustache, bald head, black onyx earrings and a choker bone-colored cross at his throat. Wedding band on his left hand, and three large jawbusters on his right and I swear one was a skull. Green eyes, almost pale. He arched an eyebrow.

"Okay, yeah, hi." I tried to sound cool.

He gestured to the empty chair.

I was a little embarrassed about banging the door, more than a little unnerved, and he didn't sound welcoming. Cool was a bust. His presence was intimidating, and I screwed up my social courage. I stuck out my hand and reached over the desk.

"Clem Reeger. I left a phone message yesterday, but didn't get a call back, so I assumed silence was consent. I pass this place all the time." I didn't add that I first thought it was a head shop.

He smiled broadly, stood and took my hand with a firm, strong, and near knuckle-breaking grip. "I'm Boo-Boo."

I laughed and gave his fist my own death clutch, and he chuckled with me.

"Boo-Boo?"

"Yeah. You should've seen my man Yogi."

I settled into the folding chair and we gave our respective biographies. Mine was pedestrian and routine and I added that I was separated and newly retired. In a deep calm measured tone he told his tale, exciting and uplifting. Boo-Boo was a Ranger with four tours under his belt. He never mentioned wounds or medals and talked expansively about his wife (the real Yogi, and we laughed at my surprise), their five kids from college to kindergarten, and he made me feel like I was an old friend.

His desk had a cup with pens, a blotter with stained coffee cup rings, and colored construction paper, probably artwork from his youngest. The real treasure was behind him on a folding table. A slew of framed photos, with varying sizes and colors, pictures of family and soldiers, solo shots and groups. In the center was the large family portrait, with Boo-Boo seated, and one daughter with a ribbon bigger than her hair sat cluelessly on the lap of a grinning but proud lady who had to be the infamous Yogi. The child was a wisp of a girl who could not have been older than five or six, with a wide gap-toothed grin, clearly the baby of the family. The four boys of various ages were positioned as sentinels around man and wife, the tallest boy standing behind Boo-Boo with his hand resting possessively on his father's shoulder. Son proud of father, father proud of son. All seven were gloriously beaming, happy and impish, especially Boo-Boo. I smiled at the photos, the real history of this man, and felt a pang of regret.

"Why are you here, Clem?"

I told him I wanted to help and thought I could volunteer with *HHH* but needed to know more. For a second he appeared off guard, but he recovered.

"Don't take this the wrong way, but I need hikers, man. Real mountain humpers. We do walks for some folks, but we challenge our clients to do the Crooked Hooker."

The Crooked Hooker, an inverted triangle on a map, had three distinct legs, making for a perfect two-night three-day commune in the high country. It started and finished at the same spot, and traditionally everyone went in the same clockwise fashion. Serious hikers, college students competing, stoners, loners, faith-based retreaters, families, and lovers all had good manners and exercised common sense. In over 30 years I have not once heard of a crime up there, which is probably owed to the open carry laws of the state.

But it is a challenge. The first leg is about 16 miles, most of it on an uphill incline, with washouts and gullies to make it challenging. We called it the "Bent Femur" for some unknown reason, and it was both tricky and boring and not sturdy after rain. The prize when you hit the base camp was a spectacular sunset, and the trick at this time of year was getting there early enough to make camp, scrounge firewood, and claim one of the half dozen generous platforms for tenting. If you were late, you might not get close to the central firepit, or worse, sit next to some kid with a mandolin. But for everyone there, the view was what it was all about. People get married up there. Judith and I pledged ourselves to eternity on a purple sunset without a cloud decades before, aided by a heavy skin of red wine. About two-thirds of all hikers camp and return to base the next day.

For the intrepid who wanted to forge ahead, after the Bent Femur the second day is all about the "Broken Hip," as miserable a climb as any for those seeking just recreation. The leg itself was only six miles, but it was nasty, constant up and down, mostly up, no cross-hatching possible, and at several wretched points hands were required, and knees, too, for the winded.

The camp at the end of the Broken Hip is communal. Too steep to forage for firewood, there is one large pit and a wide plateau for campers. A few years back, long after I stopped making the climb, I heard they beat down some brush for a helo rescue pad. I was both relieved and deeply concerned knowing that.

The last leg, day three, was mostly downhill, a cross-hatch of 14 miles. Easy stuff, compared to the Broken Hip. It's called many things, most of it colorful, but the one that sticks is "Silky Smooth." The path is wide, soft dirt, no obstructions, and the steep downhill parts have stairs cut into the hill. Ironically, more people get hurt on the Silky Smooth than the Bent Femur or the Broken Hip, simply for taking the relative ease for granted. It was tough on the knees but I thought I could hack it.

I was well aware the Crooked Hooker was arduous and not to be taken lightly.

"Boo, look, when I got out of the Corps I did the Crooked Hooker once every other month, it seemed. Even after I started up with Judith, she and I kept up the pace. We have some great and miserable memories there. I have a pal who used to muscle it with me back then. You may know him, Coach B?"

He brightened. "Yeah, met him a few times at the school. Good dude."

"Boo, I know the Crooked Hooker." It came out as a plea.

"When was the last time you humped it?"

It was clear that my vice-like grip and casual sweatshirt did not hide a puffy expression and early 50's paunch. "Maybe, seven or eight years?" I knew it was more like fifteen-plus.

"You have to be fit, Clem, but that's only part of it. Our clients are former soldiers, marines and sailors who have some level of PTSD. They are fit, sure, but they carry some heavy packs around every day, at home, at work, at church, everywhere. Their triggers are different, their pain acute and largely unseen." His gaze was direct.

I wanted to sound tall while seated. "I thought your clients were, you know, amputees." It came out as if my being physically whole made me better than his people. I cringed inside, but I wanted to hit this head on and did not want to be dismissed.

He smiled, nodded, and inhaled deeply. "Not really. Our amputees are guides, for the most part. I know it may sound strange, but I don't worry about those guys. They need to be challenged, sure, but they're smothered with love and attention, and are real heroes who have adapted to their new reality."

He paused, shifting in his chair, concentrating. "The amputees we see are medically stable and don't need proximity to a VA facility. They do see themselves as still somewhat invincible, and love a physical challenge."

"Like the Crooked Hooker," I said, finishing his thought.

"Yes, but more so. There's a cool group called Phoenix Patriot Foundation operating out of Texas and San Diego that sponsors high risk events for amputees. Mountain climbing, long distance jet skiing, paragliding. Fun and dangerous stuff, man. Good group."

"But not your, uh, market."

He leaned forward. "Right. People walk in here with emotional burdens of their own, or are referred through our social network locally, like VET-CITY. Another cool club I network with."

"I've heard of them. My company hired a bunch of people through their efforts." Even though I was fired, humiliatingly, I was still proud of the place.

"So we engage the referred or walk-in PTSD soldier or airman or marine or sailor. That's why you have to be in shape. If there's an incident, or meltdown, out on the Hooker, you can't be sucking wind or nursing your own blisters." His eyes bore into my chin.

Boo was right, of course. But I kept forging ahead. "Let me show you my commitment. I can get it back together... I want to help, Boo. I must help. This is why I am here now, on this earth, I know it. I have the true motivation. Let me help. Please." I leaned into each word.

He seemed to be getting older during our conversation. I originally pegged him at mid-thirties when I saw his physique, but I mentally scribbled through that and put him ten years older. Easily.

Boo smoothed his eyebrows with one massive paw, the small gray hairs bouncing back, the smaller reddish-brown ones laying flat. He stared intently at his desk calendar, which I suspected was more show than commitment. He appeared undecided. We settled into a long silence as he considered my worthiness. Normally I would have ended this dance, but today I wanted his approval more than I needed air to breathe.

"Sorry, Clem. Just thinking about a good fit for you." He kept playing with the calendar.

"Oh!" My relief and excitement was evident.

"Look, man, maybe nothing before Thanksgiving, which puts us into spring. They close the Hooker for the winter, and I'm not one to mess with Mother Nature or the Park Police." It was early October. He probably thought I needed a lot of gym time.

He inhaled sharply and held it.

"I have a client. Good kid, will be doing his, uh, two-week reserve drill with us. He returns on the 25th and expressed an interest in going out on the Hooker. What do you say?"

I was stunned. "You mean, me and him? In like three weeks?"

"I'm thinking the weekend of the 31st, through Sunday the 2nd. Gives you almost four weeks. And it's conditional, dude. I'm your final judge and arbiter. First, start walking with weight. Ease into it but don't take time off, unless you're injured. I want a verbal from you daily."

"Good, good, I need that, Boo."

"Second, and this is my problem, is that I need to find a third hiker. Always two to one ratio. Might be tricky as most of my guys are committed. Without a third there's no hike." My impression was that he didn't have a lot of backup to begin with.

"I understand." I didn't agree, though. Never a good poker player, my thoughts came out of my pores.

"This is to protect everybody involved, Clem. I'm taking a big chance on you, and Arlo, my client, is a special guy. This is not debatable." I had the sneaky feeling that he could grip my neck, shake me like a maraca, and stuff me in a dumpster right then without breathing heavily.

Yes, Boo-Boo was the scariest human I have ever encountered. I squeaked my agreement.

@@@@@

Run. Walk. Run. Walk. A lot of walking. I had four weeks to get ready and I had no excuses.

It was still before 1000 and I wanted to hit the ground running. Walking. With weight. The weather was perfect, a little cool that required a sweater or jacket, but I knew I would cook off if I didn't prep right. I threw on sneakers, comfortable shorts, and a long sleeve t-shirt. I had two ten-pound barbell disks in an old rucksack and two bottles of water. After searching for my ball cap and shades I was ready to walk the neighborhood in a three-mile loop that I knew from years back. It was not ambitious and I didn't want to strain anything.

I was in terrible shape.

I was okay for the first mile which was generally flat. I shifted the rucksack at least every third step and began to perspire. My hat was hot. By the second mile I had drained both bottles of water, not because I was thirsty but because I rationalized that my pack would be lighter. My feet were on fire, my knees felt like uncooked macaroni and I had to use a toilet, sooner rather than later.

One loop. Three miles and I was home. I made the head call. I took one of the weights out of the pack, changed my shirt to a short sleeve, and ditched the hat. I had committed to at least two loops today, maybe three. It was just walking. I left the house and started round two.

I replayed the conversations of the past few days and my failure to defend myself better, or at least to be comfortable in my own skin. I thought a great deal about Judith. None of it was her fault. I was resolved to win her back, but she was delicate and the damage I caused over a lifetime of my immaturity was potentially irreparable. I would have to do a better job listening to her cues, verbal and non-verbal. She was more than worth it.

I made it into the third loop, without incident and without lightening my load. About halfway through I felt the distinct rawness of a heel blister. I checked it out and it was a doozy, broken and bleeding. I did not bring anything for this eventuality, the last time that would happen, ever, and I begged the Heavens to send me a sign of what to do.

No sign, so I called an Uber.

Once home I performed the required first aid. I had to go out the next day and report to Boo-Boo. I knew I needed help to get in shape without killing myself in the process.

I called Billy and laid it out for him. He was curious, sympathetic, supportive, and told me to put myself into his hands. He brightened when I related the *Heroes Who Hike* story and meeting Boo-Boo, saying he would've dragged his knees over broken glass just to see my face. I asked if he wanted to come over to watch football and he begged off, laughing that he had a hot date.

We agreed to meet at the gym the next day at 1100. I raised my feet, watched some football, called for a pizza delivery, and put a small dent in a bottle of Macallan. I thought I earned it.

I fell asleep on the couch with the TV on.

5

OCTOBER 5

My phone rang, near my head. It was 0700.
"Hey, Silly, you up and at 'em?"

I caught my breath. Judith hadn't called me that in years. It sounded like she was up for hours. My feet throbbed in time to my head.

"Hey, Judith, you okay? It's early."

"Yes!" Pure Judith, shockingly intense when she was excited or happy or disappointed. She was happy now, thank heavens.

"I was thinking about you after we talked the other day. This could be a good thing for you."

I coughed and started to mumble and sat up, but she burst forth.

"Did you watch the *Old Timers* last night?" She was enthused and I smiled with her, picturing her eyes bright.

The *Old Timers* started as a garage band from our town, a little younger than us but not by much. Twenty years ago a decent bunch of musicians started a club which morphed into rock band imitators that secured some bar gigs. They were pretty good. Judith and I followed them around town and into the City a couple times to see them play for years, and then about ten years ago they started getting warm up gigs for Really Big Names, like Billy Joel and Elton John. *Old Timers* even had a couple original songs, and one became a mega-hit, "Same Kind of Different."

The front man played a fair lead guitar, but he could sing anything and had great range and presence. The drummer was the real showman, and a bass guitar, keys, and a saxophone rounded *Old Timers* out. A shy woman played a box guitar on a stool to the side, and three other ladies who couldn't be more different in size and shape shimmied and performed remarkable harmony and backup. Big band.

But one hit begged another, and they just didn't have it. All had other jobs or households, but if you watched one performance you knew where each of their passions lay.

They enjoyed hanging out with each other. Performing, between songs, the after parties. They were a special clique and they knew it. Everyone gravitated to them, at least us locals did.

The drummer was a savvy dude, a brash, kinetic man who was always perspiring and wiping his brow with a handkerchief, reminiscent of Louis Armstrong. More importantly, he had industry connections. He pitched and sold a concept, the story goes, and the *Old Timers* now had a number one hot TV show property. In its inaugural season, after only three shows, the whole country was watching Saturday nights at 9pm. And couldn't get enough. Of re-runs.

The *Old Timers* were re-performing old TV shows, iconic ones that screamed of nostalgia. The shows were not adapted or changed at all; they were identical in every way to the original. Same script, same camera angles, same everything including the credits. The first show was *The Honeymooners,* and six members of the band had roles, the only people on screen.

Critics loved it. Viewers talked about it incessantly. Magazines were dying but had the *Old Timers* on their covers. Network TV started running the original shows. Talk shows featured members.

The Rifleman was second and had one of the band's teenagers play the kid.

"Perry Mason was last night, Clem. Did you see it?"

I asked Judith who played Perry (the drummer) and who played Paul (one of the backup singers) and Tragg (box guitar).

"The gender change was hardly noticeable. Della was the lady who does the solo songs, the one who sings "Same Kind of Different." And the tall shy one played Detective Tragg straight and she really pulled it off. Now I have to watch the original show to see the difference! Oh yeah! They murdered Billy Joel!

"*What?*"

"No, in the show."

"Was Billy Joel in the show?" I played along.

"Acting! He was the rich guy everyone hated."

"Who hates Billy Joel?"

She giggled. "Stop it! You know what I mean."

"What's the next show?" Her eagerness was alarming and I wanted more of it.

"*Twilight Zone!* And there's no tip-off on which one. Two of the band members haven't had speaking roles yet, the bass player and the really pretty backup lady. I can't wait!"

I smiled with Judith and was amused as she never really cared for current TV, through nearly 20 years of being together. As if reading my mind, she pushed on.

"I really enjoyed the old B&W shows, and these are so cool 'cause we kinda know these people. I'm so happy for them." My Judith.

We went back and forth about the *Old Timers* for old time sake, and we hummed our way through awkward pauses. I circled back to Boo-Boo and the *Heroes Who Hike on High.*

"You better start getting in shape, Clem."

We agreed to meet for lunch on Tuesday and, after the appropriate first aid repair to my heel bandage, with that wind in my sails I laced up my Saucony's and started walking. With ten pounds. I wanted to be sweating when I met Billy at the gym in a couple hours, plus I had to focus on a purpose for living better, yet all I could think about was the drummer from the band playing Ralph Kramden. Judith said that if it was possible to be better than Jackie Gleason, this guy was it.

6

OCTOBER 7

The day was rainy and cold, matching Judith's mood. I had selected an artistic salad and tofu place for lunch farther than we used to roam that I thought she liked as she once said to me way back when. Turns out management had changed twice, and it was on the border of a greasy spoon with organic greens, not a good combination.

Out of the blue she started in on me.

"I really think you should not hang around with Fat Tick," her arms folded and her chin up.

Fat Tick was a fixture in the community and not for the right reasons. He had a reputation for outrageous behavior and over the top antics which most people laughed off as embellished gossip. I knew better.

He was enormous in height and girth, mostly girth. I guessed he was Samoan or Hawaiian or an Island-ish mix, and even though I was a mere part-timer in his entourage, kinda semi-annual, all he did was clap my back, call me little buddy, and pay the freight for the evening. Since I always picked up checks this was refreshing. I have known Fat

Tick for almost ten years. Billy refused to be associated with him.

Fat Tick was loud, vulgar, and dominated the space wherever he went. Two long legged ladies usually clung to him like accessories. If he had a source of income I didn't know it, and although we never said more than a couple words to each other we were tight since the first time I met him.

@@@@@

Years ago I was coming back from a hard night drinking too much in the City and got a flat tire on the interstate, which was a Godsend since I knew that driving was a crime in my condition. Going through the motions I began the slow process of the work of changing a flat, first dumping the equipment from my trunk and then discovering I had no earthly idea what I was doing.

Lights flashed and a horn blared. Although kneeling when it happened the sound and light threw me off balance and I fell, hard, into gravel and mud and a deep brackish puddle. I started cursing loudly at the night.

A huge shadow covered the headlights of a stopped vehicle behind my car, followed by booming laughter rumbling like distant thunder.

"Whoa, little buddy! I didn't mean to startle you!" Music blared from the vehicle, a stretch limo. I assumed the giant was the driver, so I took it out on him.

"You scared the crap out of me, man! Why'd you have to blast the horn?" I struggled out of the ditch, wet and rank. "Why'd you have to lean on it?"

"Yeah, that was uncool. I'll talk to the driver about that." Traffic was slowing to gawk at us, even in the dark.

He was big and beefy, in a fat way, jowls that hid his neck, blending his head and shoulders into one indistinct mass. He was wearing a tux and looked damn good despite being disproportionate. I bet he hadn't seen one of his own ribs since the first grade.

"Man, you're a big dude," I slurred, "Pick this car up for me and I'll throw the tire on and I'm outta here." I laughed stupidly at my own wit.

He got to one knee and asked me if I knew what I was doing.

"Nope. Guess not."

"Look, my little friend. This is what we're going to do." I listened with the drunken intensity of over-compensating to focus.

The giant called Triple-A and invited me into the party compartment of the limo. At least three slinky women, and I swear a dude who was a pro-athlete or celebrity were laid back on plush leather, chatting and smoking and drinking.

I was sobering quickly, and demurred because I was wet and stank to high heaven.

One of the ladies inside shouted through the open door, "Then strip, Cowboy!"

So I did.

My new friend laughed the loudest.

"My man, you're funny." Huge dazzling smile.

"I'm Clem, Clem Reeger." I stuck out my hand, naked to the world, horns honking as they passed.

"I'm Fat Tick. Now get in the car." He put a massive paw on my shoulder and shoved me in the door and that's when I noticed the blue and red swirling lights. I tried to shrink into the seat.

"Turn down the music, bud," Fat Tick said to no one in particular. He strode directly up to the cop car. The celebrity rolled down a back window of the limo.

"Hello, my brothers!" Fat Tick bellowed, happy and friendly. I thought of running, I thought of shouting for help, I thought we would die in a hail of bullets.

We could see the cops greet Fat Tick like an old buddy, the big man using fluid gestures clearly telling a tall tale about my shenanigans. I was screwed.

In about a minute the cops seemed satisfied, got in their vehicle, cut the lights, and eased into the night.

Fat Tick stuck his head up to the window. One of the girls chirped, "What did you tell 'em?"

"The truth, sugar, the truth. Most of it, anyway."

Triple-A came, fixed the flat, and left, all managed by Fat Tick. They put out a flag and markers to highlight my car, as I was in no condition to drive it home. The party went to my place to drop me off. I didn't have any wild stories to tell while the music cranked back up. The celebrity gave me a near empty fifth of Jim Beam to put over my junk while the girls teased me to take a swig. When the girls started kissing each other I made sure to keep the bottle in place.

Fat Tick thought it all hilarious.

The next morning I called Billy to help me retrieve the car as Judith was angry at me, again. Billy gave me an earful about Fat Tick: he was bad news, he's on the police radar, he has questionable business practices, he was a despoiler of youth, corrupter of all good and decent. I thought it was overdone and told him so.

"He saved my ass, Billy. If he hadn't come by and stopped, or if I was outside of the car when the cops rolled up, I would have been arrested." My new friend was my hero, though I could not fathom why he would help me during what appeared to be an outrageous road trip.

@@@@@

Judith and I ate in mostly silence, punctuated with small comments and unenthused purring about the nice looking but bland food.

I had mentioned at one point of us living together again, if she could picture that in our future as we had been apart for a year and it was killing me.

She turned her head slightly, lips pursed, and swallowed, "We never really lived together, Clem. You had a toothbrush at my place. I wore your stuff at yours. You don't want that commitment, and please, don't bring it up again. It upsets me."

I leaned over the table, desperate for her attention and I asked her to give me a good reason, something I could fix.

"Clem, you don't remember, but when we broke up you hadn't brushed your teeth in two weeks." I winced. I did not remember at all.

We finished our lunch and she made an excuse about an appointment, leaving before our coffee arrived. We didn't talk about Fat Tick again.

7

OCTOBER 9

I saw Mrs. Yoga Pants every day during my ruck-walk in the morning and afternoon. I did like seeing her and I suspect she might think I was stalking her, so I did nothing more than "hello" or "beautiful day" or "getting chilly."

She had a great figure, brilliant smile, and seemed perpetually happy. Her dog was friendly, too. Mrs. Yoga Pants gave me an opportunity to talk to her on my neighborhood walk yet I always hustled past, thinking about Judith, thinking about getting into better condition, thinking that she was a siren and I would be dashed on the rocks like Ulysses.

Today Mrs. Yoga Pants stood at the corner with her hands on her hips, tight clothes, ruby red lips surrounding alluring white teeth. Big Jackie O shades covered her eyes and as I approached I sensed they didn't match her smile. I was walking right toward her and I would have had to stop just to get by her.

"Oh, hi," a drawl, indiscriminate and I couldn't identify. It dawned on me that Mrs. Yoga Pants might be stalking me.

I stopped two strides from her, defeated. I silently vowed to ask her out.

"Hi, I'm Clem. Clem Reeger." I stuck out my hand.

"I know." She didn't reciprocate. The nice dog, sitting at her heel, was at rapt attention. I made a clap gesture and rubbed my palms together.

Her tone was abrupt, "I wanted to ask you something." I let her get it out. I was breathing heavy, anyway.

"Your neighbor, your buddy, Mr. Jackson. How long have you known him? Is he married? Does he work? I mean, what's his deal?" She rotated her hips once, spandex catching the light.

She purred "Mr. Jackson" in a very nice way. I didn't know if she was being offensive or intrigued. Her posture toward me hadn't changed much, still argumentative, though I detected her eyes might be twinkling behind the sunglasses when she said Game's name. I zagged to her zig.

"Why don't you ask him? He walks the neighborhood, too." It came out like an accusation.

Her head snapped back and the dog recoiled. Maybe it came out too aggressive, but I was tired, sweaty, aching, and my routine was interrupted by this formerly friendly currently controversial woman of ample distractions.

Mrs. Yoga Pants then softened and the dog curled behind her feet, with the saddest eyes.

"Oh, Clem, I can call you Clem?"

"Sure, if I can call you something..."

"It's Heather," and she extended her hand. When I took it, my hand clammy and wet, she twitched just a little, and said, flat and without emotion, "Not Mrs. Yoga Pants."

My turn to lurch back, but she gripped my hand like a vise and started laughing, a throaty trill that was real sexy.

"Don't be embarrassed. I know you more than you think! I've been dating Game for, well, three dinners and I know nothing about him! All he does is listen to my silly stories or talk about you or his son or the Army." She drifted to a stop.

My mouth open, all I could say was, "What?"

Mrs. Yoga Pants, Heather, kept chatting, her preferred and natural state. My mind reeled. I didn't know they were dating and I sure as heck didn't know that Game had a son. He and I had been in each other's kitchen, foyer, patio or deck, only, neighbors for at least 15 years. I had never seen a photo in his house, and it was not likely he had seen one in mine.

Some buddy I was.

I had a sudden twinge in my side, and almost panicked. I needed to make a head call and I was a solid five minutes from my home. My face could not hide my discomfort and Heather, my new friend, wiggled her fingers and quickly walked away as I marched toward the house and relief.

These workouts were taking a toll.

8

OCTOBER 11

I picked up Billy at the gym after 0900 and he was sweating extra hard for a Saturday morning.

"Thanks for driving, Clem. You do a ruck today?" I told him I had.

"Good. I ran here about two hours ago, mostly in the dark. I would've called you anyway, but I wanted to motor, Slim. Couldn't slow it down for you, no offense. So, what is it we're doing?"

Billy breathed easy and even though he had just showered he was perspiring through his shirt.

I told him I wanted his opinion of *Heroes Who Hike on High.*

He grunted and we kept our thoughts to ourselves for the short drive. The day was overcast and unusually balmy. The air was beginning to thicken and clouds cast a certain pall over the parking lot as we pulled in to an uninviting lot, met by a glowering shadow that made the strip mall look filthy, used, and worn. It was as if seeing the decay of it for the first time. The shop windows were dirty, the sidewalk was crappy, and garbage, broken asphalt, and weeds punctuated the parking lot.

Billy picked up a few scraps as we walked from the car to *HHH*, anything that was in his path. He could never help himself. I waited outside the door as he delicately dropped the trash into an overflowing receptacle on the curb. We entered, him clapping his hands and wiping them on his jeans.

"Gentlemen! Sit down!" A command, but Boo-Boo seemed genuinely happy to see us both. We shook hands all around.

"You're Coach B, right?" Big smile from Boo.

"Yeah, Boo-Boo, we met at one of the VET-CITY events." Billy's grin was his usual *I'm cool and I know it.*

"I remember. Great programs you have at the high school. My son is Ian Callahan."

Billy brightened. "Oh, yeah! Great kid. I wish he stuck with baseball. Decent arm, good power."

Boo-Boo appeared delighted to hear the compliment. I might as well have stayed in the car.

"Yeah, thanks. Ian is a great kid. He has new interests, just not playing ball right now."

They went back and forth for a few minutes talking high school baseball. Billy knew the eldest boy, too, the one with his hand on Boo-Boo's shoulder in the portrait. As if on cue, he picked it up and admired it unabashedly. Billy and I both could have been in the parking lot then, it would not have mattered.

I was happy about the camaraderie, but was anxious as to my status, and wanted to get on with it.

"I'm ready, Boo. Been working with the coach here and I hope I haven't dried out for nothing," I let the slight lie float in the room.

I thought I was being funny, but until Billy laughed Boo sat impassively, and only then did he smile with dimmed eyes.

"It's only been a week, Clem. No one gets ready that fast, even a Marine." I think he expected me to take the left-handed compliment and walk out happy.

I leaned forward. "I have three weeks to go, Boo. I can do this."

Although his posture was non-committal, Boo went back to playing with his desk calendar as he had a week prior. He wasn't reading now; he was stalling.

"I don't have a third, yet, Clem. Sorry." The apology lacked sincerity.

It stung. I was torn between fury and begging but froze until Billy threw in.

"I'll go," Billy stood. "Been working with Clem this past week, and his commitment is solid."

Boo eyed him steadily.

I regained my composure. "Look, Boo, this isn't K-2 we're talking about. I know the Crooked Hooker..."

"Me, too," said Billy.

"...and I know I can do this. Bring it on."

Boo nodded. Without looking he picked up what appeared to be a stray sheet of paper from his desk. "Here's a list of basic gear. I suggest you don't deviate." He held out the paper to me and I grabbed it. He wouldn't let go.

"Can you meet our client, here, in two weeks?" Boo-Boo growled and I nodded. "Good. Weather permitting, the three of you will do the Crooked Hooker in three weeks, a three-day turn, starting Friday the 31st." He let go of the paper.

I stared at it. I didn't have most of this stuff on the paper, and I swear that Boo and Billy were snickering, a thought that passed in a second. Those two shook hands and then Boo stuck his paw out to me, the one with three jaw-breakers on his fingers.

"Welcome to *Heroes Who Hike on High*, Clem."

As Billy and I walked to the car, I balled up the gear list and started giving him grief.

"I'll go? Just like that?"

He cocked his head to the side. "Yeah. You've motivated me, my friend. Let's do this." He stopped walking.

I stared at him, humbled and grateful and a little annoyed we didn't discuss it before the meeting with Boo-Boo. My anxiety fled knowing he would be there.

"I don't have half the crap on here."

"Gimme that." He unfolded and eyeballed the list, and began reciting: "Socks, first aid kit, large knife, small blah blah, poncho, e-tool, fire starting kit, 2000 calories a day blah blah, shelter half and bag and cushion and water and tablets and weapons optional..." He looked at me and shrugged with a look that announced *what's-the-big-deal?*

"Okay, Slim, let's go shopping..."

9

OCTOBER 14

I met Judith for lunch at a diner where I took some of my meals, for the second time in as many weeks, and told her of Boo-Boo and the list and Billy tagging along.

"Sounds like fun! Do you know the client?"

"No, but we meet in a week or so. Between Billy and me it should be no problem." I professed a confidence I did not feel. I had stuck to my ruck and walk routine twice daily with conviction, and the aches and rashes and bone pinching were not wearing off, especially since the weight workouts with Billy were thorough and painful.

We both ordered salads. Judith remarked that had never, ever, happened before.

I nodded. "With all the crap I have to carry, the less weight the better." I held her gaze and whispered, "Your hair looks nice, Jude. Classy."

She beamed. "You noticed! My, my."

She wanted to talk about *Old Timers*, and the recent shows: Twilight Zone and Gomer Pyle. "Gomer Pyle was both stupid and hilarious."

"It always was, right?" I stared at her mouth.

"I know, but just seeing the frontman doing Jim Nabors was too much. And they finished with all of them singing *"America the Beautiful"* a capella."

"Yeah, yeah, I did see that on the morning shows. Really amazing."

"Yep! Their first departure from the oldies, but they had to come back to their brand, you know?"

"You're beautiful, Judith." It just came out, I had to say it, and I couldn't take it back.

"You're sweet, Clem." Her face clouded. "Really, but I'm not ready yet. Please."

I wanted to lighten the moment. "I could die on the Crooked Hooker, babe. I had to tell you."

She laughed, that wonderful silly sniffling laugh.

I was feeling agile and wanted to ask about something that nagged at me.

"You haven't mentioned your art. Are you working? Teaching? We talk about these nutty TV shows, but not about you." I kicked myself for not asking about her, first.

"You forgot my dog Baby-Face."

I slapped myself cartoonishly on the forehead. "Hey, you know what I mean." I put my hands flat on the table, ready to hold hers if she needed consoling. *A Face on the Flag* was rumored to be short-listed to the Smithsonian, but Judith wanted to create, not just collect royalties. I felt for her and I wanted to be her rock.

Her eyes widened, soulful and warm, and welled with tears. Happy ones.

"I got a job offer."

"Huh?" My eyes popped open.

"From a university. In Wisconsin." She was animated and excited and couldn't get it out fast enough. "They want me to teach art as an elective, really open up liberal studies. I have to conduct two 100-level art history classes, and two or more art "labs" of hands on techniques with non-paint or ink. I'm a name for them, and they're an outlet for me. Higher level. Okay money. Beautiful college town. And they want me. Want. Me."

"But, but, but, Judith, it's so cold up there!" I couldn't hide my distress.

"So what? I'm terribly bored here, Silly. No, not you, but unhappy with where my career is, and well, not very happy we're apart."

"Hey, you wanted the separation." Too strong.

"No, Clem. You wanted it. I asked for it."

"I don't get you…"

"That's the point, isn't it?" Her eyes flashed and I pulled my hands up and away in surrender. She stood up abruptly.

"Wait, Judith, please. Wait."

"No. You don't take this seriously until I bolt, and then you're all charm. Save it."

I stood. "Judith, please. I am happy for you. It sounds like a perfect opportunity. Almost."

"Almost?" she arched an eyebrow and folded her arms over her chest.

"Well, what about me? Us?"

She shook her head, sighed, and looked tired, a different woman than the one who entered the diner.

"Go on your hike, Clem. We'll talk when you get back. Be safe." And she left. I sat there with my mouth open until the busboy cleared the dishes and started wiping down the table.

@@@@@

I pushed through shin splints, calf cramps, swollen knees, and a thousand phantom aches and pains, hating every second of it. My days were spent eating, walking with at least twenty pounds, a sprinkle of running, lifting, squats, fluids, a little reading, some TV, and generous napping. I ate ten Chondroitin a day.

I was close to being depressed and I knew it. The exercise was keeping me from complete despair. I might have stopped it all if not for my commitment to Boo and *HHH* and to Billy. Billy was saving my life and his approval had always been important to me.

Billy told me early in the process, "Here's a cardio and weight workout program for you. I do think you should meet me at oh-five hundred, daily, too. You can shadow whoever I'm working with. The variety will do you good."

He was right, of course. By the end of the second week, I was feeling real progress, especially my wind and my quads. I had reported maybe a dozen times over the phone to Boo-Boo, and though he was far from encouraging me each time, he did not pull the plug.

10

I sat at a corner table at the Chop House in our town, farther south than I care to go but it was a respectable place for a blind date. Before this month began, I went to a high-end dating site looking for companionship and without predators of either sex. Judith and I were ice cold when I made the arrangements. I went through the agency's rigorous screening process, which was more of an endurance test of my patience than anything else. The beauty of it all was that the ladies paid for the matchup. The pre-date "not a match" rate (my term) was 70%-plus for the guys. I passed the online hurdle and two lengthy phone interviews.

My perfect match was meeting me at 1900 at the Chop House, and although I generally sniffed at the place, the food was above par, the service overall good, and the drinks generous. And it was dark. I felt that I was forcing myself to get through a date I made a couple weeks ago that I forgot about. Nothing wrong with a platonic getting-to-know-you.

A lovely woman, a blond, at least ten years younger than me entered, saw me, waved, and strode up to the table I was seated at. Normally I don't notice clothes, but hers were fashionable, form fit, and showed her figure in a soft, feminine, and mature manner, a maroon dress suit with grey kerchief and other accents. I felt a pang of guilt because Judith would have been impressed.

I stood, and her smile was friendly and confident as she stuck out her hand in an assertive open fingered reach. Firm shake, all eye contact over a pleasant smile, as though rehearsing for a job interview.

"Clement?" Eyebrows now arched, green eyes. Her figure was subtle and athletic and I considered that I was punching way above my weight class. Strong eye contact, and I double clutched the suave greeting and audibly swallowed.

"Hi, Trish. Just Clem, please."

"So nice to meet you, Clem." She took her own chair and scooted into it before I could pretend chivalry. Trish beamed.

"Thanks for meeting me at the table. I didn't think, well, the bar is kind of tacky to first greet," she sailed.

"I agree." I was still standing and folded into my chair. "But a pre-dinner cocktail wouldn't hurt," I responded, wanting to appear more regular-guy. "And I'm starving. How about we get some appies?"

She laughed, cute and throaty, saying the right things and I felt happier than I had in ages. We ordered drinks and a big shrimp cocktail for two. That was my last moment in this paradise.

"So, Clem, I know the agency does its homework thoroughly, but, if you don't think it's impertinent of me, what are your assets?"

Up until then she took my breath away. Now I exhaled from the haymaker I didn't see coming.

"Excuse me?" I heard her fine. I was stalling.

"Look, Clem, you seem nice and all, and there are minimum standards, but mine are not. I have been burned a few times, and ..."

Then I noticed the crow's feet around her eyes, the grey hairs near her temples, a few poking through in the part in her hair, the lips which were full and red moments ago were now pinched and thin.

"Trish." I gave my best imitation of a patient sensitive man.

"Yes. Oh, you're offended." No apology, not empathetic. Her eyes unfocused and I sensed a retreat from her, back to being a woman on a blind date.

"No," I said, "I'm not offended. And I read your profile, too." I was not angry, but certainly disappointed. "Just divorced after nineteen years of marriage. Gotta be tough."

"It is. Was." Her glow clouded.

"Two kids in high school, who are probably taking advantage of the situation. And you're just getting back into the job market."

"I am," she offered, initially hopeful and realizing I was no longer flirting. "And it's been difficult. We have a social status that can't be maintained. My business skills are outdated and I can't make them work for me today... they're over 20 years old. My kids cling to me; I got the house, right?" She nodded and slumped.

I filled the silence. "But they're spoiled and now are pals with dad and you're the heavy. You liked being married." I thought it sounded sympathetic, yet it came out harsh and judgmental. I suspected she'd take the bum back if he'd have her, but I sensed a hardness about her that would likely have prevented any reconciliation by either party. I shook my head and exhaled.

"Look, Trish, can we start over? How much money I have is not a good topic on an empty stomach. Please."

The drinks arrived, two very dry and dirty martinis. Trish grabbed hers, mouthed "Cheers" and whipped it down in one shot, crushed olives and all.

"Nope. I'm done. Done. Thanks." She got up and without another word or gesture strode toward the front door.

I stared at my drink, furious at myself for not being gentler. I sipped the martini, smacked my lips in appreciation, and the oversized shrimp cocktail arrived. The waiter guessed or observed my predicament and had the good grace not to comment.

I was doomed to compare everyone to Judith forever.

It took me 15 minutes to finish the shrimp and order a second cocktail. Another quarter hour of reflection and I felt like a new man, though a lesser one, telling the waiter that I might have dinner at the bar and to close out my check.

The Chop House bar is nice all by itself and many people meet there at Happy Hour, though on a weekday night by 2000 it thins out fast.

Trish was sitting at the bar, alone at the far end, not wanting to be noticed. Assuming she had been here since she left my table, she was easily into her third, if not her fourth cocktail. I walked up to her, hoping she would see my approach before I had to say something. Her perfect 'doo scooped low, and with her head bowed her hair almost touched the bar.

"Oh, you. Go away," she mumbled.

"Trish, look, I'm sorry I overreacted. I feel terrible."

"Go away." Louder. The bartender approached and asked if there was a problem.

I wasn't going to let the barkeep control my conversation, here, or let her get away with making me out to be the bad guy.

"There's no problem, bud. A misunderstanding. I'm apologizing." I said to Trish, "May I sit down? Trish?"

She didn't answer and the barkeep walked away, out of earshot but close enough to clobber me, if it came to that. Trish just shrugged. I sat next to her, casual but not too close. I caught the bartender staring at me, so I gestured to give me what she's having and refill hers.

He brought me a martini, but only for me. I took the hint. She scowled at both of us.

"What do you want?" I imagined a slight slurring from her.

"Want to take another shot at dinner?" I gave her my best nice guy smile.

"No. But listen. I'm a good girl. Always. True and loyal for over, well, forever. Perfect home, some bumps. I starved myself for that jackass, and he throws me over for some girl, like, five years older than our daughter!"

She was getting loud so I murmured, "So sorry, so sorry."

As if a switch was flipped, Trish sobered. "Joe. Can I have a coffee, please?"

I smiled at her, but I was forcing being kind. She aged in less than an hour. Her make-up was still in place but there was lots of it, getting blotchy. Judith never used make-up, except a little lip gloss, like she was daring me to kiss her. Trish's lips looked caked in wax.

She swiveled in her seat. "I'll be right back," grabbing her clutch she glided to the rest room.

Joe the bartender came up to me. "She slammed three of my drinks in, like, 30 minutes. You her date? You stood her up? Or just late?" He was not friendly, not even a little.

"Nothing like that. What's the tab?"

"Forget it. Second time this month she's here. Last guy didn't show. Doctor emergency, at least he called. I had to listen to it all. Nice lady, but she shouldn't chug..." I cut him off.

"Yeah, I know. Let me settle." I gave him three twenties. "Leave us alone, please."

Trish returned, cheerful and sheepish. The coffee came.

"Clem, I'm sorry. This has been difficult."

"Yeah, I get it. But you have nothing to apologize for, Trish. I went through a breakup a year ago and I'm still messed up about it." I gave her another good friend sad smile.

She sighed heavily. "I kissed a couple frogs, Clem, who turned out to be lying liars. That's why I went with the service. Which is far from perfect, thank you very much." She sipped her coffee.

I suspected that was a dig at my photo, which was ten pounds and a lot of grey hair ago.

I felt for her, but I needed an exit strategy. If Judith could throw her life at a rescue dog, I might be susceptible in getting trapped into being a protector of a woman who didn't like me. We sipped our beverages in silence.

She cocked her head and smiled. "So, how much money do you make?"

I had to laugh, and she brightened.

"Trish, enough for me, but not enough for you."

She looked away and nodded long and deep. "I get it. Let me finish my coffee and you can walk me to my car. I'm okay now."

Ten minutes later we were walking to her car and there were two sixty-somethings pawing each other against a Mercedes, an older C-class, really sloppy kissing and grinding hips like teenagers. They were both awkward and responsive and oblivious to the world. We had to break up the party to get Trish into her vehicle. We were more embarrassed than the couple.

"Oh, wow, I'm sorry. I got carried away," the gentleman murmured to his date, which seemed like the right thing to say to an embarrassed paramour.

"No, oh, haha, that's okay. Really." The lady gathered her hair. "Um. Fun, I mean, fine."

They walked in opposite directions and all Trish and I could do was look away and share the private joke, the first time we enjoyed something funny in unison since we met earlier.

"Look, Trish, I'll call you. We should do dinner, do it right."

She deflated for a heartbeat, smiled, and squeezed my arm in her strong hand. "Yes, Clem, yes. I'd like that." She spun quickly and entered her car. Trish backed out slowly, and I stood still, waving awkwardly at her while she was about a foot away, putting her car in gear. She grinned without teeth and nodded and pulled away.

I called Judith on the way home. No answer, straight to voicemail. I knew she was still upset with me, but I told her I missed her, I needed her, and I hoped she'd call me. I tried to say something thoughtful about her dog but it came out phony and pathetic. I hung up wishing I hadn't left a message in the first place.

In bed at 2130. 0500 would come fast.

11

OCTOBER 20

J udith called me in a rush mid-morning with real excitement in her voice. I took it for a good sign knowing full well that every time I got my hopes up I would just fall harder. We met for lunch at a diner she likes, sweet potato pancakes served all day, one of her favorites.

Judith couldn't wait, jumping right into her story before I slid into the booth.

"You know, I had dinner with him last night," she said, leaning forward for effect.

"Who?"

"Fat Tick!"

"*What?*"

"Yes!"

I stared at her, shock and disappointment mixing with my imagination. Fat Tick had a notorious reputation with the ladies, and although he was at least a decade Judith's junior, she still had all her charms.

"Clem. Breathe. It's not what you think." She looked concerned, probably because I looked awful. I wore my emotions on my sleeve.

"I know this guy," I stuttered. "He's, he's..."

"A perfect gentleman," as she arched an eyebrow.

I arched one back. "Oh, c'mon, Judith. How can you be so naïve?"

"Okay, smart-ass. You know he's an accountant?"

"*What?*"

"Yes! Look, some of the license agreements for *A Face on the Flag* are expiring, and I mentioned to Billy, you know, I needed help."

I knocked on the table. "Billy loathes Fat Tick. He's a terrible influence on young people!" My voice was rising and attracting attention.

"Shush, just listen, okay?" She was getting red and that heat was directed at me. People at adjacent tables made a show of not eavesdropping or staring open-mouthed.

My head drooped. I had to control myself and strained my eyes forward and could only see her hands.

"Billy talked to Marco who apparently knows Chuck Chunco, you know, the drummer from the *Old Timers*." She said it quick and matter-of-factly.

"*What?*"

"I know, it's crazy. But get this," she rubbed her knuckles into the back of my hand, "Fat Tick is the accountant for *Old Timers*... I'm pretty sure he's their business manager!"

"*What?*"

"Clem, honey, is that all you can say?" She looked at me like a third grade teacher trying to get the attention of an excitable child.

How could I explain that I saw everyone around me as having noble, even heroic, attributions? I never put Fat Tick into that group, but if Fat Tick was a legit success on the ascendancy, what the heck have I been doing with my life? I hung around him on occasion because I was getting low, a too often preferred state for me. But was it him getting low. I didn't have a grasp on my presumptions of others, and I was staring at my own descent and lack of worth.

I also had a terrible secret about Fat Tick, one that would have brought him and any associations with him down. Judith kept prattling away, and I caught the gist of it.

"Fat Tick is really smart. And charming, but in a professional way. He mapped out a strategy for me and offered to negotiate all my contracts going forward. Make them perpetual. I told him about the Smithsonian and everything and he'll get ten points on all contracts he touches, what he called his little sweetener," and she winked at me on that point, and I saw Fat Tick leering at her when he probably winked at her initially. She was waving her hands, fingers splayed, and I saw she was imitating the way he told a story, but she didn't realize it.

I know her voice when she's happy, sad, gonna cry, gonna laugh, wants to eat, sleep, drink, and make love. I know her voice. And most times I never listened. Judith even gave me a card once, years ago, to "The World's Worst Boyfriend."

I was listening now. Her ruddy complexion was from excitement and I prayed silently that she would forget my initial jealousy and pick up on my sincerity.

She paused. "Isn't that amazing?"

Staring straight at her, I told her it certainly was amazing.

"So, with all that time you spent with Fat Tick, how come you never knew he was an accountant?

That he's a real professional?" It came out of her like an accusation.

I couldn't tell her that Fat Tick was his own guy and every now and then he let me tag along. I wasn't his friend. I was an infrequent mooch who got to play with his entourage. Maybe he needed an older guy with a paunch to round out his crew twice a year. I didn't think he knew my name, calling me "little buddy," which I hated but accepted to be accepted.

And we both had something unspoken of on each other, something meant to stay that way.

"He said to say hi," she sniffed. "Said you're due to get low," in a voice trying to imitate him.

I cringed, but with a ray of pride. Fat Tick did know my name, who I was. And that could be bad.

12

OCTOBER 23

I had hit the gym early under Billy's eye and then spent two hours doing my "ruck-cardio" around the neighborhood, the highlight of which was bumping into Heather and her dog. She noticed I was trimming down, but no mention of Game. She asked to join me soon. Good for my ego, but bad for my training, so I remained non-committal.

I got back to the house before nine, sweaty, gassed, and feeling good. The phone rang, and it was my firm's HR manager. She wondered when I would be dropping by the office.

Sooner or later I had to return to box up my belongings, and in my mind I chose later. She asked gently if three weeks was enough time, and after a snide comment on my part she said she'd be happy to box it all up and ship it to my house. Today.

I told her, a little intimidated, that I would be there by 1000.

The HR manager, a real pro who understood what the gravity of my departure would mean to the troops, informed me that the word was out that I was retiring effective November first. She threw in that I would have an intern assisting me and that all the boxes and whatnot would be shipped for my convenience, to which I mumbled my appreciation.

I walked into the shop about 1030, and as the floor shift had just returned from a break I was fortunate to only have to wave to the shop employees, who were all smiles and thumbs-up. My humiliation at getting canned was only my own.

As a founding member I had good second floor digs: large bay window, my own small conferencing area, hard walls with no glass except the door, and I even had my own head, an accidental perk when our fledgling firm started leasing the space nearly 20 years ago. Mahogany bookshelves behind my mahogany desk, and a long lateral wall with dozens of photos and plaques old and new and a few USMC mementoes. A couple plants were still in good shape, better than I had ever kept them. My domain was sparkling clean.

I snuck into my office with an audible sigh, not realizing it was occupied.

"Hi, Mr. Reeger!" A young man, early twenties, was building boxes on my small conference table.

When I saw his face a wave of imbalance hit me in the chest and radiated to my hands and my neck. Blinking several times, I grasped his extended hand, not in greeting, but to steady myself.

"Sorry to barge in, sir. I thought I could set up some boxes for you." He kept a firm athletic grip on me. "I'm..."

"Steve Spaeth." It came out like a croak. A flood of memories, good and bad and long buried.

"Why, yes! Uh, no, I'm Scott. How..." He released my hand. I was looking at a ghost.

I struggled and partially succeeded in regaining my composure. "You are the spitting image of your father, an old friend, Steve Spaeth." I stuck my hand out again, which he gripped anew and we shook with vigor.

"Oh, I am happy to hear that, Mr. Reeger." He spoke in a rush, just like his father. "I did two years of college and decided it wasn't for me and I report to Great Lakes to start Navy boot camp in January, so we – my folks and I – asked if I could intern here for a couple months, you know, learn the business of business, that sort of thing, maybe work the floor. I always wanted to work with my hands, college and book work aren't for me, so here I am."

Scott finished so abruptly I couldn't register an adequate response and I kept staring at him. He was Steve's flawless doppelganger. Here was my old friend and partner in dreams deferred who died twenty years ago.

"It's okay, Mr. Reeger? Me being here?" He took a step back.

"Jeez, kid. Is it okay?" I hugged him then, hard and awkward, so he didn't see me forming tears. He clapped my back and hung on. I broke it, and placed my hands on his shoulders, assessing the son of Steve.

"Wow, Scott. Just wow."

"Yeah, how about that, right? My dad, uh, mom remarried when I was three, step-dad I guess but he's always been my dad and he loves her and has been great to me, even if I wasn't always great with him, he got me an interview and said I should learn from you. Mom was real specific about that."

"Really, why?" I smiled, flattered and suspicious.

"Well, you know," Scott had some of Steve's mannerisms but an immature confidence, and his words flowed too quickly to process, "I think she blamed all his friends back then, when my father died. But she mentioned you as a successful guy who made good even after..."

"A misspent youth," I whispered.

"Yep. She put it differently. No worries, Mr. Reeger. None. Life goes on, dad says." We stood in a dreadful silence.

Steve Spaeth, a Navy vet in his own right, and I invented the T-Cup together. Before we could create or test or patent a prototype, Steve died in a car crash, coked out of his mind. All we had together were drawings on bar napkins, theories, but we had fleshed out the T-Cup applications and the future and drew it up almost by accident. We were both running a little wild back then, me drinking, him cocaine and its nasty cousins. Steve told me, two days before he wrapped his car around a tree at 100 mph, that his wife threw him out because he dropped his eight-month old son on the floor, on his head, the young man standing in front of me now, a face I saw every day for two decades on my wall. Steve's wife, and I forgot her name, told him it was either the family or cocaine.

He chose cocaine and told me so. Steve confessed, between sobs and a crazy look of glee, that from the first taste of that shit he was hooked, that coke and crack was all he wanted. I did nothing. I couldn't, or at least I told myself that I couldn't. Steve was gone.

I got dizzy. The kid helped me sit down. Scott had no idea that I kept the drawings, found a tool and die guy for the prototype, scraped every dime I had and patented the T-Cup which became a household staple, created a good living for hundreds all over the world, and made a few millionaires.

Like me. The kid didn't know it, and his Mom, Linda, I remembered now, also would not know. Steve was too far gone when we hatched it, and he would not have intimated anything coherent about it at the time.

"Are you okay, Mr. Reeger?" Scott looked confused and concerned, a look I saw decades ago in his father, Steve's look of fear.

I coughed, hard, and managed to walk over to my mini-fridge, grabbing some bottled water for the two of us. I drank mine deep in one shot. He stood, uncertain if he should speak or go get help.

"Tell you what, Scott." It came out hoarse. "Let's get this junk boxed up so we're not here 'til midnight."

We worked steadily in silence and banged the books into boxes and taped them tight, not reviewing most titles. I don't think I ever read one but did receive almost all as gifts over the years. I asked Scott if he wanted any of them, but he demurred at first since he admitted he didn't read much, though he grabbed two baseball books by Hall of Famers.

Except for a couple files and my day-timer, I threw everything from my desk in a box for the trash.

"Ya know, Steve, maybe we'll just put the pens and stapler and scissors and stuff in one box and bring it over to the procurement folks. Everybody needs pens..."

"Scott, sir. I'm Scott." A sweet patient kid.

Entering the second hour we started taking photos and plaques off the wall. I would grab it and he would wrap it quickly in thick brown paper and load in a box. I commented on each photo, and

I was front and center in all: this one the mayor, this one the governor, that one with a ball player, another mayor, another governor, and one big photo of a movie starlet whose name I always got wrong and was corrected, every time. Scott oooh-ed and aaah-ed on cue for everything he wrapped.

There were many plaques from organizations that were self-serving for me or an homage to our company's civic and charitable support. I threw those out.

Except one. I coached ten-year old Little League one year, as a fill in for a sales rep whose wife was ill. I kept the team picture mounted in a plaque. We lost more games than we won, and although I liked the kids and the game just fine, by mid-season I went into a funk. I was not likely to have children of my own, and Judith, the love of my life, said she didn't want them. I would forever be kid-less and I decided to forever avoid kid things, except when Billy invited me out so I could get some "fresh air" in a sweaty high school gym watching volleyball or basketball. I kept the few Marine Corps things I had.

By the time we got to the last framed photo in the most prominent place on the wall, I was starving, and Scott's stomach was audibly rumbling.

I saw Scott's face in that photo, next to mine. At a loss to say anything, I considered not handing it to him, but my hesitation may have spoken volumes.

A men's softball team from nearly a generation ago, youngish guys with the name of a bar on most of the grimy shirts, untucked, unkempt, in the standard shot kneeling and standing behind a modest trophy. Billy was in the middle, kneeling with his hand on the prize. He earned it, too, as our shortstop, number three hitter, and captain.

Standing on the far left was me, technically the short-fielder, though I knew they hid me on the weak side of our outfield to suit the hitter. Next to me was a strapping and fit athlete with longish blond hair, wearing a well-worn Navy half sleeve sweatshirt, his forearm resting on my shoulder, a pal's gesture of possession and camaraderie. He was talking to the camera, saying something I could never recall, while the rest of us mugged for the shot.

It was Steve Spaeth, Scott's dad, less than a week before his car wreck and death. A dead ringer, I reflected, regretting even thinking that.

I looked at Steve's face every day I was in that office and anyone who entered it for more than a minute saw it, too. It could not be avoided. Most people commented that I must have loved the pic because of its ideal viewing location. And I was in much better shape then.

Scott dropped the paper wrap and stared at his reflection.

"Wow, Mr. Reeger, I don't have anything like this. My mom, well, she showed me baby pictures and I can't remember the last time I saw her wedding picture or anything with, you know, my father. He, he looks like he's in motion, so alive, so, you know..."

"Vital. Yeah. We had the world by the balls, then, Scott."

He couldn't stop smiling at the photo in awe, and I had to force myself to look at it.

"Hey, is that Coach B?"

"Yeah!" I was too grateful for the shift. "Yes, it is! He hasn't changed much, right?"

"Except for the hair," he chided. Everyone busted Billy's baldness, his Mr. Clean shaven daily head, without fail. "Mr. Reeger, he was a great coach. I had him for freshman baseball. He and my Dad, well, my step-dad, got friendly, too. They still talk on the phone."

I coughed. "So, Scott, you say your mom remarried?"

"Oh, yeah. I was like three-years old. I don't remember it, but Chuck Chunco was always my dad, you know? Great guy, loves my Mom like crazy, taught me about sports and music and we even worked on cars but we could never fix anything. A great dad. They never had other kids, Mr. Reeger, but I don't ever recall them discussing it." His eyes never left his father's face.

"Chunco? That's so familiar."

He laughed. "It should be! He's the drummer for *Old Timers*."

"*What?*" I could not mask my shock.

"Oh, yeah, quite a ride. I have to tell you, he spoils me and mom. I mean, it's embarrassing. The only time he was ever, and I mean ever, sore at me is when I told him I joined the Navy. Wow, he was pissed. He wants me to stay in school."

A warm shower of relief fell on my head, shoulders, my back. Steve's family didn't struggle while I padded my bank account. Scott probably knew of Steve's addictions, but told in his mom's way, and it was not my story to tell. But the resemblance...

He had no idea that I cheated him and his mother of a proprietary interest in T-Cup. My guilt began to evaporate like sweat off a mule. It was still there, and it stank to high heaven, but it did turn to cold mist and begin to disappear.

I got away with it. After all these years, and all I could think about was me, not Scott or his mom, and not Steve, who spent the last seconds of his life coked out and crashing his car in a horrible wicked useless death.

"Mr. Reeger, can I have this picture?" He looked me dead in the eye.

"Oh, sure, but... show your mother. Ask her. If she balks get it back to me. If you can't display it, I will."

He smirked at me, like I was an old fool, and I deserved it. "I'm an adult, Mr. Reeger. If you allow me to keep this, I will give it the respect it rates."

It was all Steve. His way, all the way, and on impulse I blurted out, "Please, son, whatever you do, stay away from drugs. All of them. You don't know..."

He put up his hand and shook his head, and although the gesture was a firm rebuke his eyes were kind.

"I promised both my parents that a long time ago, sir. My dad, Chuck, my real dad, also had his own problems and I am right in the head with it all. My mom still worries, yet nothing has ever been past my lips or up my nose and never will be. Now, can I have my picture?"

I said nothing, and he seemed satisfied with that, and slowly turned on his heel and out my door. Scott was hypnotized, seeing himself in a man he didn't recall, and eager to show his mother his find, that of his uncanny likeness to a man I cheated after death and who I once called friend.

I waited for a few minutes staring at the nail-pocked wall, assuming that he was making a call or hitting the head. It took me half an hour to finish all the taping and stacking and he had not returned.

Luette entered and asked if I was ready. I told her to have the freight shipped to my home and in the next breath I inquired, fumbling apologies, if she was okay.

"Oh, Clement, I am. I'm now the CEO's personal administrative assistant. Got a nice raise, too!" She laughed, teasing me. Things were looking better for her already.

"That's great. I was concerned for you." A lie, and she knew it. I had treated her poorly for years. "Say, did you see where Scott, Scott Spaeth, went?"

"That good-looking hunk of man? He left. He was smiling and kinda weepy and I asked him if he was okay, and he said he'd just received the coolest gift ever. And he kept walking. I gave him the business, my best flirty stuff, but he didn't nibble. Did you know his dad is Chuck Chunco of the *Old Timers*? Everybody follows their shows, just amazing! That family is like royalty, rolling in dough!"

I shook my head at her. "Well, thanks for everything, Luette," as I walked away from it all.

One cure, if possible. I was getting my ruck, adding weight, and putting in another couple of miles.

13

OCTOBER 24

A long glorious Friday and after a hellacious workout and ruck, I was pacing hours before meeting Judith for dinner, our first real date night out in over a year.

I showered and shaved and put on a favorite sport jacket that Judith had bought for me from a thrift store years ago. At the time I laughed when she did, thinking about who might have croaked and the kids who gave it away. It was a forest green tweed with faux wood buttons and leather patches at the elbows. No matter how much weight I gained it made me look slim and cerebral at the same time. It was snug at the shoulders but at least I could button both front buttons and I knew that Judith would be impressed.

I was more nervous than I should have been before a dinner with a woman who was the center of my life for nearly 20 years.

I wanted everything to be perfect and would have settled for simple contentment. Judith and I have eaten at every high-end place that has endured or faded away in a thirty-mile radius of our town, but a new Italian place opened up, midrange prices, generous portions, bring your own wine. No pretense, which I hoped would impress Judith, and I spent a good bit of time arranging for the right table, right view, and got a reservation at a place that didn't take them. Fifty bucks and a handshake go a long way.

Everything would have been perfect except the table next to us was pushed against two other tables for a rowdy group of parents and kids celebrating only God knows what.

My eyes shot daggers at the proprietor, who shrugged his best *outofmycontrol* stance and palmed my fifty-spot back to me, real contrition in his eyes. I took it back and nodded.

The boss, Sal, was going to be our waiter and he was most solicitous and gracious, especially to Judith, who was immune to his charm. In my own annoyance and disappointment I had not read her mood well, at all.

Sal worked the oversized Chianti bottle I brought, when on an unseen cue the adjacent table burst into "God Bless America."

I almost said something, they were that bad. But another table joined in, and soon everyone in the place was singing, and Judith's mood lightened. Even Sal waved his arms like a conductor, butchering the words, and before a third chorus could start he exclaimed with a smile, "Your food is getting cold, no more singing!"

"Clem, do you still love me?"

The cacophony was still a low rumble, like distant thunder now, threatening to come back over my head with a vengeance. This was a bold opening from her, and I choked, leaning forward as if I couldn't hear well.

Sal came and we ordered the same dish on his recommendation.

"You heard me, Clem." Her smile, the best one, the one I would gladly die to see just one more time.

"Yes, yes," I croaked, and swallowed hard. "Of course, I do, always. You, you're all I really have."

"Clem, I don't know where to start and when I do I don't know if I'll be able to finish." She put her hands on her lap but kept her eyes locked onto mine.

She whispered over the din, "The more I try to find meaning in my life the hollower it feels. And much of that is your fault." Not an accusation. Stated as fact.

"Hey, Judith, I'm..."

"Please don't cut me off, Clem." She shot Sal a glare as he approached and he flinched as if struck and then retreated.

Judith continued after a deep breath. "If I can't share what's good in my life, why enjoy it?"

I didn't know if I should answer and she plowed ahead.

"And you have bad in your life, Clem, the kind of bad that you caused yourself. If you're not in a bad place, you put yourself there, into a small hole and make yourself hopeless and I know you are better than that. And you won't share it or change it. I know you treat women like accessories or worse, and you treat me like a little girl." She sat straight up and lifted her chin imperially.

"I am a gift, Clement. I am."

I reached for her. "Oh, God, Judith, I know. I am in awe of you," I said, fighting tears.

She pushed on. "I am tired of being independent for the sake of it. I never wanted that. Oh, I know I never wanted marriage or kids, but I want to be the center of your life. I don't want a drinking buddy. I want a man." She sat ramrod straight, mouth a thin line, hands hidden, eyes boring a hole in my forehead.

I wasn't floored or shocked or flattered or chastised. I was defensive.

"You really want to know how I really feel? Judith, are you settling for me? Aren't you always disappointed?" I was in earnest but didn't want to go any deeper. The gnocchi came.

Her eyes softened, and since she didn't reach for the chow I didn't either. "I don't know why you sell yourself short, Clem, especially to me, and why you lack drive and initiative and ambition and purpose to the whole world! You phone it in, well, you have, for years, relying on, banking on, an old process to keep paying you. That isn't work, Clem. You're not even a caretaker of the T-Cup. You're a hired hand."

"Not even that anymore." I stared at my cooling gnocchi, eating far from my mind even though my body screamed for it.

She was losing steam. "Well, I hope this hike thing works for you."

I ventured leaning forward, "Helps us. I know it will."

She sniffed and shook her head slowly. "You don't get it. Look, Clem, what do you really want? What's your purpose?" It came out like a hiss.

"Judith. I want you. I never wanted to be great. I just want the means to be happy." We had the ambition talk a hundred times. We never got anywhere with it.

Her eyes widened as they do on this subject. She cocked her head, and sang sarcastically, "Are you happy?"

I slumped and said no.

She stuck out her arms and said too loud, ungently, "Then why not try to be great?"

I waved for the check to hide my embarrassment. Sal was mortified about our untouched dinner and I reassured him, giving the fifty spot back along with payment and a too generous tip. If I couldn't maintain my dignity with the only person whose opinion mattered, I would lord money over a hard-working stiff trying to please us. I overpaid to boost my mood but I left feeling petty and small.

We walked outside in silence for a block, aimless in the night chill, our jackets hunched to cover our necks.

I had to break the ice. "You, uh, hungry?"

Judith laughed, a trill, a little forced.

She gripped my arm in both of hers as we walked.

I snapped my fingers. "Hey, Jude, what's up with Baby-Face, your new dog? Where's he at tonight? Caged?"

She stopped dead in her tracks, tightening the grip on my upper arm. I feared the worst, but she was calm.

"I had to give him back!" she said. "And his real name is Pumpernickel."

I began to laugh but stopped when I saw that old flash of anger. I was the only person in her line of sight.

I tried to recover. "But I thought it was a shelter, a rescue dog..."

"Yeah, me, too. The shelter called me and said it was a stray with an owner and that a little girl was missing her dog, yada yada. I had to bring Baby-Face back, and for a Bassett Hound it flew into that girl's arms. I walked away."

"But you didn't cry."

"No," she sighed, "I did not. I am a terrible mother. And kinda relieved." She started walking again.

"Hey, Clem." She paused, gripping my arm tighter still, maybe from the cold, maybe from...

"I got the job offer. In writing. To teach. At that college."

I wanted to be delighted. Judith really is a talent and I told her so.

"Well, first, the Smithsonian has committed to display the door, too. My door."

This was something to celebrate, but I couldn't resist. "*A Face on the Flag* door?"

She stopped. "No, my back door with the broken latch. Yes, of course the *Flag* door. There's some haggling over whose name goes where, but I have 100% control of the art and I'm all in. That's part one."

My stomach growled and I thought Godzilla had risen it was so loud.

She gasped. "What the hell was that?"

I let the rumble subside. "The antipasto. Not bad, huh?"

She groaned. "Hey, the ice cream place is two blocks over. Let's go there."

We quick walked and were the only two patrons when we arrived. It had a sign it was closing for the winter by the 31st, a week away.

Judith laid it all out for me. Her job offer to teach in Madison was now solid, about a million miles north.

"It's a beautiful college town, Clem. Wonderful," she said. I had never been there.

She had been approached by the University for a permanent position primarily because of her work and her name but an endowment of ridiculous proportions was set up in the School of Arts with only one stipulation: that Judith be hired (if she desired) in whatever capacity she wanted. The endowment was that big.

"Some benefactor. This guy knows you?" I was impressed and very curious.

"It's a she." Judith told me a long story of her being in a dance class since we split up a year ago, a class I never knew about. When I questioned that, I must have sounded jealous.

"Don't be a nitwit, Clem. Ladies only. Exercise and socializing for seniors. I'm the kid in the group, honestly."

She told me her partner for most of the weekly sessions is a sweet little old lady in a walker. I struggled to contain my surprise, and if Judith saw it she let it slide. Now I knew where she was all those Wednesday nights.

"Mrs. Grandsen, Louise, is a force of nature, Clem. Sharp as a tack, worldly and knowledgeable about so many things, including dance and art. My art. She really has a tough time getting around, and the dance class was the highlight, maybe the only light, of her week." I could picture Judith dancing with a lady in a walker, giggling and gabbing and just being happy.

"About six months ago I began picking her up for class, which quickly turned to dinner and a real friendship. It filled a small part of the vacuum of you not being there. She lives very modestly, maybe too much so, a widow for decades."

Then the real story. Mrs. Louise Grandsen was the Salsa Mamba Queen of Wisconsin and Minnesota, if there was such a thing, back in the 50's, 60's, 70's and into the 80's. When her husband passed she moved to our City to be near her children, who within a few years all moved away.

"Jeez, Judith, that's so sad."

"I know. She takes it better than I have."

"But even a salsa whatever queen doesn't have that kind of money, Judith." I shook my head.

"She's got it, Clem. Been selling records since the 50's, and her cut is generous. There are dance lesson tapes on reel to reel and those are now on disks and YouTube, and she gets a lot of that, too. She never spent a dime of it and told me she'll be damned if any of her family gets it."

"Now that's sad."

"I know." She looked down at her empty bowl. "So, there it is. The endowment names an art room after Mr. Grandsen and I'm now sponsored. A kept woman." Her smile would have crossed the planet. "There's a little more to work out, and Louise says she'll take care of it, between the Smithsonian and the School of Arts, but there you have it."

I asked her why Madison, why not local.

"Oh, yeah. Weird. Her late husband was a UPS driver in Madison. She said those were the happiest years of her life, raising kids, and them travelling with a rotating salsa band to teach dancing. She said people threw money at them back in the day, and that her late husband would approve."

My frown was not well hidden. "When? When do you go?" I knew I could never ask her to think about it. I was dying inside but to act the jilted beau would have crushed her.

Big sigh from her, and, "I was thinking of flying up before Thanksgiving, scout the town, maybe hunt for an apartment." She stared at me evenly.

"Oh, yeah, of course." I still stung from her accusation of why I couldn't just be great. She knew I wasn't happy without her. "I don't know, it's gotta be cold up there. I mean, everything's here." It sounded weak, I felt weak, and her withering look said it all.

We didn't talk much after that. I drove her home, and after arriving as I started getting out of the car, she put a hand on mine.

"Go home, Clem. You're in training," with a wan smile.

"Oh, I, uh, coffee?" I was crushed.

"No, dear, not tonight."

I nodded a dozen times. Perhaps to stop my neck from breaking she chirped, "Hey, Clem, what are you doing next Thursday, the night before you leave for the hike? I'll make spaghetti for you and your friends, your place."

I brightened in an instant. "That's splendid!"

She got out of the car. "I'll call you for the battle-plan," she said in her terrible imitation of a Marine drill instructor growl.

I chuckled as she slammed the door to my Audi, an act I always hated and she knew it.

As I drove away I realized I had never spoken to her about my day with Scott, Steve's son. She would not understand my anxiety, and I was relieved I could keep it buried for another day.

14

OCTOBER 25

On Saturday Billy and I arrived at the mall in my car about 20 minutes early to meet our client. I had just detailed the inside of the Audi myself, and spent a small fortune having the exterior cleaned up and buffed out. I had let the car go to the dogs and I needed to make it right. It gleamed so much in the early cool autumn sun that I squinted to a parking space away from the usual cluster.

I glanced at Billy who was smiling at me, nodding and wearing sunglasses that made him look like a hitman.

"What?"

"Clean car, Clem. Smells good. Worthy of you," he kept nodding.

Exiting the car we saw a smallish but sturdy 20-something guy exit a beat-up late model pickup truck parked close to *Heroes Who Hike*. Black North Face jacket, jeans, and all terrain shoes, and a dreadlock ponytail tucked under a grey ballcap with a logo I didn't recognize. Dark features, he walked like an athlete with a leg injury, but sprightly, directly to the *Heroes* door like he owned the place.

I couldn't see inside just yet, but I guessed that he was our client and was chatting up Boo. I was anxious to meet him.

Billy said the obvious, "That's gotta be our man."

We entered, and the kid was sitting comfortably on the top of the unused desk, smiling at Boo who was in the middle of a story. They both froze.

"Sorry to interrupt, guys. I know we're early." I tried to sound casual.

Boo stood. "You're good, Clem; actually, Arlo is late." He jerked a thumb at our client partly in reproach but more so in jest. Billy and I sat in the only chairs available after shaking hands all around.

"This is Arlo McIlhenny, army vet, friend of the family. He wants to do the Crooked Hooker with you." Boo was smiling a little too broadly, the only time I ever thought he was forcing an emotion. Billy kept his shades on.

Arlo's forearms were heavily muscled, his left one sporting a simple blue tattoo of a coiled snake. No rings, no other adornment. Clean shaven except for a manicured patch of close cropped hair on his chin. The hair tucked under the cap was more wiry than at first glance and seemed incongruous. Arlo had a friendly smile, his eyes a deep brown with heavy brows.

"You ain't Irish, I guess." I was trying to lighten the mood.

It came out wrong. Rival service branches are notorious for breaking each other's chops, and I wanted our client Arlo, who seemed 30 years younger than me, to feel like he was one of the guys. I have a standard playbook of one-liners meant to show camaraderie and I usually get a laugh and a return volley equally harmless and predictable.

Billy let out some air, an "oooooo" that was patronizing. Boo shifted painfully in his seat. I kept up my grin to Arlo.

He hesitated, somewhere between a "What the ..." and "Outside, old dude ..." when Arlo barked a genuine laugh, his head shaking slowly.

"Whatever, man. No, just American."

I tried to recover, but Arlo was faster in being gracious and calmly waved his hands. "We're good, Clarence."

"It's Clem."

"No shit." Everyone laughed at that, and I tried to believe the crisis was averted.

Boo took over the meeting, all business, all three of us signing release forms acknowledging that we had the gear recommended and that after completion we would agree to a press release of the hike for PR purposes. Arlo and Billy went back and forth on timing, special gear, rations and who could cook what, and an unnecessarily long dissertation on weapons. I had not spoken since my gaffe for nearly ten minutes.

"I'm surprised you would still want me to go." I felt awful about my weak attempt at humor and had to get an apology out. Arlo spoke, Billy and Boo looking down at their hands.

"Maybe after the hike I'll have to make a police statement, then we'll worry about publicity."

Billy and Boo thought that was a riot, and I joined the joke after a second's hesitation. I suspected Arlo was a PTSD client and I really didn't know the man.

"I'm starving. Who wants to get Chinese?" Billy's first meaningful words since walking in the place. Boo and Arlo begged off, and Arlo hopped off the table, shook hands with all of us while giving me a friendly pat with his other hand, a sincere gesture of reassurance. He walked out with the same athletic gait.

"Jeez, I just..." I exhaled.

Boo was sympathetic. "Forget it, man."

"He won't."

"Prove yourself on the hump, Clem." He wiggled his heavy ringed hand in my direction. "A little shared pain goes a long way to redemption."

Walking to the car, I stopped and tapped Billy, hard, with the back of my hand.

"I don't give a crap about lunch, Billy. Maybe we should call the whole thing off."

"Okay, okay. You don't want Chinese. Jersey Mike's it is." He folded his arms across his chest.

"I'm serious, man. This just doesn't feel right anymore." I might have been shouting.

Billy uncoiled his arms and placed one hand on my shoulder. "Look, Clem. We're going. You have a big investment in getting ready. Your first impression took a hit just now. Let it go. It can't be undone. Now we're gonna forget it." He reached in his pocket. "I'll give you five bucks to keep an eye on your ego. It's not worth that much more." He laughed out loud on that one, and I had to smile despite feeling even worse than before.

"You know, Clem, Boo wanted to meet with Arlo before us. Like a briefing."

"Yeah, I guess." I didn't guess that at all, but as soon as Billy said it I knew he was right.

"Maybe Boo was giving him a lecture when we walked in, or about to. Or checking his suitability. Or warning him, I don't know." He trailed off, unusual for a guy who always knew his own space, skin, and sight line. "Maybe briefing him on us."

We ate lunch and talked about nothing. I was too internalized to appreciate the scope of Billy's thoughts. I spent the afternoon walking with a 20 pound ruck for four hours, alone, modulating my breathing and trying to change something I said that couldn't be taken back, resolving to be a better person and knowing it would take a lot more than being embarrassed.

15

OCTOBER 27

Monday's workout with Billy was sure to be most intense, but I was ready for it. My innate fear of failure and vow of personal redemption fueled my energy.

Billy commanded the gym and in between sets he was doing his "I'm the mayor" thing, the women flirtatious and the men envious. I was trying not to puke from exertion.

"This is our last hard workout day, Clem. Just squats tomorrow, then walking in soft shoes Wednesday. Easy on Thursday, and hit the ground running Friday."

I grunted under the bar machine, unintelligibly .

"Spaghetti Thursday. All we can eat." He was excited about Judith cooking for us.

Another grunt from me, a little higher in pitch.

"Hey, Coach!" It was the principal of Billy's high school, Myra. She wore a bandanna over her normally spiky hair, and with no makeup she looked a lot older. Trim petite physique; she had an aura of confidence, the kind that natural leaders possess.

"Hey, Principal Myra!" Billy all charm. "Doing legs today?"

She waved him off, addressing me. We were casual acquaintances and always got along. "Oh, hello, Clem. So, you're the cause of Coach B missing work Friday? Hmmm?" She was smiling and standing a little too close to us both, especially if I was going to hurl, sweating like a donkey notwithstanding. I stopped working, took a knee, and tried to control my breathing.

I nodded in acknowledgment. Billy answered with a grin only.

"Sorry to interrupt, boys, just wanted to be on record as against this little foray. The weather is supposed to turn on the weekend. You guys aren't getting any younger!" She spun on her toes, a little coquettishly, and I had to rethink my presumption that she didn't like men, specifically and in general. She certainly liked Billy, touching his elbow as she left.

"I thought she didn't like boys." I wanted to extend the break. I was gassed.

"Don't be a complete jerk, Clem. She's a great principal and educator. And friend." Billy leaned close as he said this, to keep me from embarrassment, but maybe to see if I needed medical assistance. My heartrate was still high and my breathing much labored.

"Myra is an Army vet, did four years in mortuary services. Not an enviable task. She then got her degree in clinical psychology and does ad hoc work for women veterans in counseling services. She is thick with VET-CITY and respected in the community. Myra's the real deal, Clem. I am fortunate she looks past my faults."

"I give, man. Let's call it a day. I'm dying here." I was tired of my own caged thoughts. I was tired of myself, not the workout.

With that, Billy laughed out loud, attracting the attention of every early user in the gym. Some chuckled with him, not knowing why, trying to be in on whatever joke was made. All Billy jokes invited merriment.

16

OCTOBER 30

I spent the day before the hike soaking in the tub after a neighborhood walk without the weighted ruck, at Billy's suggestion. The three days before the hike was without serious lifting or free weight training, just stretch and walk, stretch and walk. My feet felt both tough and supple, and my legs were as ready as they could be.

Judith had come over in the afternoon to make spaghetti and meatballs, my first indulgence with high carbs since I started the whole thing. I had lost 10 pounds and it looked it, all from my gut.

"I'm very proud of you, Clem." That smile, that small encouragement, gave me all I needed to walk to China.

The house smelled great, as Judith can make a marinara to beat the band. Meatballs the size of baseballs, and two was the limit as per the chef's orders. Judith asked me to set the table for four.

"Who's the fourth?" I knew Billy was coming over.

"Game. You told me, Clem. On the phone Tuesday. You asked him, right?"

I remembered, and I forgot to ask him. "Be right back."

As I barged out the back door Judith called after me, "Dinner in an hour!"

I didn't need to get very far. Game was enjoying the end of a lovely fall day smoking a cigar the size of a trombone on his back deck overlooking the neighborhood. I called out to him.

"Italian night at the Reeger half-way house in an hour, Master Sergeant!"

Game stood and blew out a stream of milky smoke. "A bottle of red, okay?"

"You don't have to bring anything but an appetite, Game!"

"I'll be there!"

Crisis averted, I asked Judith if I could help.

"You're a little late, Silly, but open a couple bottles of red and let them breathe." She continued to hum and said over her shoulder, "And set the table, please."

Billy came in the back door an hour later, with Game in tow.

Judith outdid herself. Normally she is not big on cooking, preferring a menu over anything in the kitchen. But she can cook Italian just the way I like it, and added the right accent of antipasto, bread, and grated cheese. It was her super-power.

Everything was delicious and we attacked our spaghetti and wine in equal measure. Billy took his foot off the gas a little while the rest of us were enjoying the warmth and intimacy.

I tried to fill the vacuum created by Billy's less than ribald attitude tonight. I snapped my fingers.

"Say, Game, I meant to ask you. I was badgered a couple weeks ago by Mrs. Yoga Pants. She started peppering me with all kinds of questions about you."

Game eyed me. "It's Heather. I know, she told me."

"I don't mean anything by it, Game. You and I have called her that for years."

"Oh, yeah, I know, I'm just as guilty, I guess." He eyed me conspiratorially. "We've been seeing each other. Lovely woman. But she does ask a lot of questions."

Judith was flushed from the wine. "Like what?"

"Well," he leaned back and dabbed a napkin at the corner of his mouth. "She wanted to know if I was married, had any kids, that sort of thing."

"Do you?" Irrepressible and innocent, Judith was not shy.

"Why, yes, Judith. I was married for a short while, been divorced since, well, I guess it's over twenty years now. Have a son, too." His face clouded.

Billy was looking at me for some reason, not at Game. It was an accusatory stare and I knew its meaning: *how the heck didn't you know this.*

Game pressed on, seemingly unaware of the drama around the table, almost talking to himself.

"The boy, well, I didn't raise him. I wasn't involved. I sent money until he was 18, but never a gift, nothing. His mother and I were on terrible terms, the kind of terms that cannot be bridged with civility." He paused and looked up from his fingertips. "He never had the father he deserved. I know he joined the Army, served downrange, too. I tried meeting him but he's, uh, keeping me at arm's length."

I asked Billy to pass the bread. Judith refilled Game's wine glass, and I swear she winked at him, telling him with her eyes, *tell us, we are with you.*

Game smiled back. "He has let me back into his life, at least we talk. I am grateful for that. I did admit to him I was lonely, and I think that softened him."

Billy asked, "His mother?"

Game pursed his lips. "She lives in New Zealand, if you can believe that. Nasty piece of business. I can't get farther away from her, period."

I wanted to change subject. "Billy, I still feel stupid about what I inferred about Myra earlier."

Billy looked directly at me, appreciating the gesture. "Look, she's great people, and I don't care who she likes. I hate to say I take advantage of her liking me, but everyone has favorites, right? All bosses, even high school principals, have favorites and she has been good as gold to me. When she first got to the school I was assistant coaching all the freshman teams in season, boys and girls. I was doing the rah-rah cheerleader bit, which only the non-athletes really appreciate."

Judith interrupted, "But Myra..."

"Right, I'm getting to that. I was exhorting the freshman girls' volleyball team before a match against a rival high school. Mind you, these girls were a mix of just- stopped- playing- with- Barbie-dolls and could- be- mommies- if- the- wrong- type has influence. Remember when you were fourteen?"

Judith shuddered with exaggeration, then snickered at her herself.

"I was giving the girls my standard fighting speech, that we must defeat the enemy or they will come into our homes and kill our families and burn it all to the ground, and that when we drink from our enemy's skulls we will taste true victory, you know, something like that."

"Billy!" Judith was appalled but could not have been surprised.

"Yeah, well most of time, in fact all of the time the kids eat it up, get fired up, or take it for what it's worth... that it's only a game, so go out and do your best. Buuuuuut... One girl screams at the top of her lungs, real primal stuff, and bolts from the classroom and runs right into the new principal, Myra, who heard it all." Billy sat back and looked at the ceiling for a moment. He inhaled.

"Myra took charge of the whole thing. She hugged the girl, told her to swallow hard and get control. Then she told the now horrified team to go out there and kick butt today, for the eyes of the whole school were on them, and they ran out onto the court. I stood, frozen, looking at my new boss, whom I did not know, and waited for instruction. Myra whispered something to the now not hysterical child, who smiled and joined her teammates. I asked her, "What did you say?""

I had heard this story a thousand times, as had Judith, who politely forgets every time until the punchline.

Billy deadpanned. "She told the girl, "Men are complete idiots.""

We all laughed on cue. Game asked, "What happened to you?"

"Myra is the best. She told me to lay off the martial stuff with freshman unless I knew the thinking of every single one of them, starting with their names. Good advice, and I have taken it to heart and lived by it. What she did so well was balance every person's needs in the moment and made it all work, positively. She's a pro, I respect her, and I consider her a good friend."

Billy gave me that look of *don't mistake our friendship for one that supersedes all others. If you're wrong, Clem, you're wrong.* I nodded that I understood without either of us saying a word.

I needed to lighten the party. "I thought this was gonna get juicy about Mrs. Yoga Pants." I put my hands up in front of Game, pretending to obstruct blows. He wound up his right fist in exaggerated circles.

We got the right reaction, smiles all around.

"Heather and I are seeing each other, nothing serious," Game said casually.

"Any sleep-overs?" Judith had more wine than I thought. Game roared immediately, and Billy and I were now intrigued.

"No, my dear, no sleep-overs. Actually," and Game looked around the room as if we might be overheard by someone not at the table, "Heather and I first, uh, met at The Dirty Martini Party."

That got a new reaction, expected and complicated. All of us opened our eyes wide and exaggerated an "OOOOOH" in unison that reached a crescendo in eye-popping guffaws.

"Oh, boy, do I remember that night," I said between chuckles. I actually remembered very little of it.

Billy threw in, "I'm still hung over from that night."

Judith slipped in, "Oh, wow, that was, what ten years ago?" She dropped her jaw when she asked me.

"More like eight, I think," corrected Game.

The Dirty Martini Party was a neighborhood scandal for the ages. A new upwardly mobile couple enlisted a few other neighbors and decided to throw a theme party for a few select couples. Roman toga stuff, with a DJ, the whole shooting match. The selection list grew and became a "come as you are" party for anyone who could make it. Everyone in a four-block area came.

There was no food, but there were two guys cranking out dirty martinis, smashing olives like a machine press, shaking ice and gin, creating whole pitchers, and pouring into plastic straight up glasses. No one had time to wonder if they would or should slow down as the booze was flowing like water in the balmy evening, a glimpse of summer weather late into the fall that we all kept remarking about. A night that made you glad to be alive, the kind that only meant bad decisions.

The DJ played a lot of oldies and I drank more than my share. I had lost track of Judith for a while, who didn't go in for martinis and was probably listening to someone's opinion about art. People started pairing off, and not with their spouses. I was propositioned by a pleasant lady who I only knew as the co-owner of a donut shop. I did not behave well, but I had buried that caper very deep in my mind.

We all glanced around the table. Judith and Billy were failing at avoiding each other's eyes. I sat frozen, and Game broke the silence.

"I ran into Heather at that party. More like crashed into her. Took her almost eight years to say anything to me, just the past few weeks. She divorced a few years ago, which I never knew or noticed." He held up his hands. "It had nothing to do with me."

I couldn't let that slide. "Probably had a lot to do with her Yoga Pants." Game and I chuckled.

Judith was looking at her hands, and Billy was gazing softly at the side of her head, her ear, her hair. I would have shuddered if I wasn't half lit.

I remembered more about The Dirty Martini Party in what I didn't see, than what I actually did that night, and it hit me like a ten-foot wave. I developed a serious headache.

My best friend and my girl were never an item, and the worst thoughts in my mind could not make that fiction of jealousy come into focus. Yet there was no mistaking that something may have happened that night, something significant but unacted upon, something that kept our tribe and friendship intact. We are all human, and we all lose our heads now and then. A crazy and stupid night.

"I have a little headache, and I need to get to bed early. Big weekend, right?" I looked at Billy for support.

"Oh yeah, Slim. We should turn in early."

Judith and Billy started clearing dishes while Game finished his wine. I stood, rubbing my temples.

"Hey, Game, thanks for coming over. I hope you haven't been poisoned." I faked mirth I did not feel.

"Go hit the rack, Marine. We'll tidy up." He stuck out his hand.

We shook, and he said good night to Billy and Judith, with a very sweet "thank you" for her efforts. She seemed preoccupied, and when Game left her mechanics in cleaning up were most business-like.

I ascended the stairs, stripped, and went to bed. After a few minutes I heard the front door open and close, Billy leaving. More noises of cleaning from the kitchen and then Judith's footfalls coming to my, our old, room.

She whispered from the half-open door. "Clem? I'm going to my place."

"Okay." I was crushed and relieved.

"Please be careful."

"I will. Hey…" My face was half-buried in the pillow.

"Yes, honey?"

"I love you. Just wanted you to know in case I die." I tried to sound funny.

"You are an asshat. But I love you, anyway." And with that she left.

I stayed awake in the dark for a few minutes while the pasta and wine did its work. There was an image in my foggy mind of my lady and my friend, the closest people in my life, wrapped up in each others' arms, fueled by the memory of The Dirty Martini Party. I knew the image was an invention of my own guilt but it nagged at me and wouldn't go away. I was as low as I could get, then. If that image had a hint of truth I could not go on. My life was a continued wreck of my own doing and if my pistol was in my nightstand instead of packed in my gear downstairs I might have reached for it.

I shuddered at the thought and knew that I had to seize my own destiny and not fall into a pit of the things I could not control.

I was dreading the hike.

17

OCTOBER 31

A rlo and Billy had their gear packed tightly and were ready to go at 0500 Friday morning at my place. My gear was ready, too, but only because Billy did it for me days ago. I winced thinking about bad thoughts from the night before.

It would still be dark for a couple hours, the sky clouding any indirect light from the stars, the unusual humidity repressive late in the hiking season. I knew of the excessive leaves on my lawn and thought fleetingly that I should have called someone to do it. My neighbors' lawns were manicured and immaculate by comparison. My laziness would drift to Game's property over the weekend while I was away. Letting down my few friends was a common practice.

I quietly put my pack next to Billy's in the bed of Arlo's truck. I surveyed the cab and Arlo noticed right away.

"It's an automatic, Clem. The three of us will fit fine up front."

"You sure Clem can't sit in the back?" Billy lived for breaking balls early.

"You there!" It was Game. "Wasting half the day away?"

Game was outside retrieving a paper he knew was not yet delivered, but making a show of his toughness by being out in the misty drizzle in shower-shoes, gym trunks, and a loose t-shirt.

"I thought you were being robbed, Clem, like those kids came back." He was looking at Billy, deliberately avoiding Arlo, who could pass for a teenager from a distance. I said a perfunctory hello and played like I was securing gear in the truck bed.

Arlo walked up to Game, stuck out his hand and gave a hearty "Good morning, sir. Arlo McIlhenny, with *Heroes Who Hike*. We're about to start a little jaunt up a hill."

Game broke into a lopsided grin, seemingly surprised and impressed with Arlo even though I believe he remained skeptical of our general ambition. They shook hands like old friends.

"Okay, young man," he continued to pump vigorously, "Game Jackson here. Say, when you get back, ask the man of the house to rake the leaves, will you?"

Billy and Game greeted each other with a wave.

"You keep an eye on Clem, there, Coach, okay? I know he's been working out, but that Hooker is a mother." We all said our good-byes.

As Arlo backed out of the driveway, I waved to Game. I was happy he came for dinner last night, the first time I had invited him for more than a beer.

I forgot to call Judith, wincing. My cell phone was on the kitchen table where I left it.

@@@@@

We seated ourselves at one of the three breakfast-and-a-cold-beer-too all day places at the foot of the Crooked Hooker, a joint called Greasy Tony's, which lived up to its name. Eggs, bacon, sausage, potatoes, and bread, lots of it. Burgers, too, which I recommend. Nothing else on the menu but coffee and canned soda. Day-trippers could get ice and bottled water, and a ridiculously wide variety of snacks and ChapStick and other junk. Greasy Tony also sold toilet paper which was overpriced, and everyone, I mean everyone, bought a roll. Superstition runs high with hikers.

Greasy Tony's was almost empty at 0700, as the weather forecast was foreboding for impulse hikers. Rain and more rain. A small family, Mom and Dad and three kids under ten years old, was huddled and barely suppressing excitement. I guessed them to be day trippers, going about two miles up to a gentle rise to the picnic and playground. The dad was chiding and teasing his kids that maybe the weather was too yucky, but that only spurred their enthusiasm.

Our food arrived and I was suddenly anxious to get moving. Arlo and Billy chomped and gabbed about their favorite parts of the Bent Femur, and all I heard was static.

Two pairs of twenty-something couples were gearing up, but the guys' enthusiasm were meeting a brick wall of one girl's annoyance. I could hear "it's going to pour" at least a dozen times, and then that young lady, clearly unprepared for a hike up and down a mountain for a couple days, folded her arms across her chest in defiance.

"Well, I'd say we aren't going anywhere," she pouted.

Billy was taking in everything while still deeply engaged with Arlo. I always marveled at his ability to listen to two conversations. Arlo studiously tried to ignore the group.

"The blond, right?" Billy knew. Arlo, without looking, started to chuckle.

"She's wearing Ugg boots, man. She never intended on going." Arlo said, reaching for ketchup.

I threw in. "The guys are gung-ho, and the redhead looks eager. I'll bet you a beer those three go and the blond leaves in a huff."

"I don't want to see any more of it, though. Head call and we're outta here," whispered Billy, conspiratorially.

We grunted assent. The blond left, her boyfriend in tow. The other couple looked relieved.

@@@@@

The sky was the color of dried glue and I wanted to peel it off to get to the sun.

We hit the first two easy miles ahead of the Greasy Tony's drama at a fast pace, just short of a double time.

After the picnic and playground area the going got steep, a crisscross washboard with a certain path through marred tree roots and a variety of rock formations. Not easy on the foot strike, but clearly defined. There was little sound except the wind high in the trees, and the rustle of squirrels and rabbits and other furry creatures along the path ahead of us. Sound carried in gusts. Colors ranged wildly and changed as the sun moved in the sky.

There was a fresh well pump at camp where the Bent Femur ended, our goal for the day. We each had two quarts of water, six MRE's, and granola bars. I was conscious of my USMC K-bar, another tool I always carried back in my hiking days, and my Glock 19. It's the only weapon I own, but I wore it like a gunslinger. Arlo had a big revolver, a Smith & Wesson Governor loaded with .45 ACP rounds, hollow-point, he intimated, strapped across his chest like he was Pancho Villa, a thought I kept to myself. I know Billy carried a Sig Sauer, but it wasn't visible.

We didn't talk for the first couple miles. I think Billy wanted to make sure we were out of earshot of the family or the happy couple. It happens a lot; inexperienced hikers stay within sight of those who appear to know what they're doing, hoping to get adopted. It happened to Judith and me a couple times, long ago.

My mind drifted to what day two would be like, as I tried to drive the irritant of my rubbing feet from my thoughts.

The immediate threat to my fat, tired body, was about 16 miles of the Bent Femur. Only two miles in, and I was measuring my breathing. Arlo and Billy started yakking which was fine with me as long as they didn't ask me any questions.

"What did you do in the Army, Arlo? You look like an Irish desk jockey," Billy chided.

We all laughed at that one, and I knew that they would never let me forget my remark of a week ago. But it was funny, now.

"Armored cavalry. I liked it a lot, too."

I kept looking at Arlo's gait. He seemed like he was walking normally, but his right calf was a prosthetic from the knee down. He didn't swing his leg like a pirate but bounced like an athlete. If I wasn't staring at the fake leg, I would have never guessed he had one. Arlo wasn't nearly winded, and I don't believe Billy ever tired of exercise. If they were waiting for me to chime in, they would have to wait until we camped.

"I was a gunner. Routine movement, wasn't even a patrol. We never saw any indication of an IED, and two guys lost teeth from the concussion when they landed. We were lucky, for the most part." Arlo paused.

"Losing your leg doesn't seem too lucky," Billy said without irony.

Arlo chuckled. "No, I guess it doesn't. A real fluke. Unsecured weapons and unnecessary equipment caused a crazy ricochet chain in the Bradley. I went up in the air, straight up, I still remember thinking to just keep hold of something, you know?" He breathed deeply, twice. "When I came down, a sharp hunk of metal cut through my shin bone. Then the vehicle bounced again, and my leg was hanging by a flap of skin. I knew I was injured but I didn't know how bad until Shaw, my buddy, started puking."

"Oh my God." I stopped walking. We all did.

"You got that right, Clem. You have no idea what disgusting is until you see someone puking, with blood and teeth, all over the place and he can't talk and can't communicate. I actually asked him if he was all right, and he grabbed the bad end of my leg. Tried to put it back, man, I'll never forget it. His front teeth are missing, he's heaving, and I'm still trying to scramble up to the 50 cal, outside. In my mind I was pulling the trigger and raking everything in sight." Arlo paused again, wiping his brow with a bandana. The Governor on his chest rose and fell.

"There were two vehicles behind us, and I could hear shouting and the LT was right there, then the medic, and we were scrambling to get out, to see who was hurt and how bad. My leg just dangled from the skin and we thought the guys inside were in real bad shape. After the all-secure, I sat on a hunk of the Bradley like I owned it. Someone gave me a cigarette. I never smoked in my life. The medic had applied a quick compression tourniquet. They were all over me, all about my leg. All about my leg."

Arlo looked into where the sun should have shone and smiled. "All good, now, you know? I thank God how lucky I am. Surrounded by real professionals, great soldiers. All of them. They saved my life."

Billy almost reached out to touch his shoulder. I willed him not to. He dropped his hand. "Glad you're here, Arlo. Glad you're back."

Arlo gave a mock salute. "Yeah. Me, too. Hey, if we keep stopping, we'll never get to the first camp in time to set up shop before dark."

Without a word we pushed on, Arlo now in front.

The impending rain cast an invisible blanket over the surrounding scrub. No birds or rabbits or squirrels, no sound, no rush of grass. The pall of the sky was like a gauzy tent keeping direct light diffused and away. Billy had his beat up bugle strapped to the top of his pack, which gave me something to focus on without thinking about nature's unforgiving temperament.

@@@@@

Oh Say Can You See?
Any Bed Bugs On Me?
If You Do...

 # Pick A Few... #
 # And We'll Have... #
 # Bed Bug Stew! #

@@@@@

We told stories, some real whoppers. I would have preferred silence, but Billy and Arlo seemed to be competing for who had the best wind. Billy sang his stupid ditty to the tune of the Star- Spangled Banner. The stories ran into each other and my mind drifted in between the words and images.

We spoke of moonshine and crazy women and good and bad commanders, corpsmen and kings. Rarely was anyone, from the DI to the commandant, just okay. Candidates and captains were either magnificent or awful. We spoke of friends and people we lost, and that those who left before us, regardless of the reason, were all heroic in their own way. No one plans to evaporate that day. I came to think only dull people walk away unscathed, that the great and noble always died young.

@@@@@

The DI is trying not to laugh.

The recruit looked green and couldn't answer the simple question, "What's your major malfunction?"

And he starts stuttering, then Boom! He pukes on the DI and passes out!

The whole squad starts to puke, and the one behind 'em.

Yeah! The scuttlebutt had bad water and another recruit crapped himself.

We got a whole day off in the middle of training!

@@@@@

The two of them were dueling telling stories and I was happy to listen to the silliness of it all.

Billy could see I was getting gassed and he had little sympathy. "Tell Arlo about the *Salty Dogger* fight," he jabbed.

I launched into it and it came out fast.

"We were new butter-bars and thought we owned DC via Quantico," I began.

Marco had a girlfriend who became his wife, and her father, a former Navy officer, owned a small hole in the wall bar in DC with an upstairs head. Marines and soldiers and sailors went there, usually with dates or looking for them. Loud music, fair bar food, and the beer and wine was cheap though the well drinks were overpriced. We liked the place because we could usually get a seat and meet women close to our age.

"One weekend night sometime midway through TBS, the Marine Basic Course for new officers, Billy and I bombed up to DC and we were becoming suitably smashed and thoroughly obnoxious. Marco was already at the *Salty Dogger*, his girl's dad's place, and Billy and I were parched like camels in the desert and were running real hard downhill.

"There were three Navy dudes, lieutenants, I think, who looked soft when compared to Billy and me at the time. They started giving us crap in tight quarters, probably because Marco flipped them off. People generally avoided Marco and took it out on collateral targets, like me.

"I went upstairs to the head, guys right, ladies left. I walked into the familiar spot: one sink, one urinal, one crapper, fumbling with my belt, when all three Navy dudes walked in right behind me. I spun, my junk exposed, with my hands in front of me, and the first guy slipped on the wet deck and went down hard. The second one shoves me and I bounce off the urinal, but still on my feet.

"Billy bursts in, picks up the third squid, and shoves him headfirst into the stall."

I have to pause telling the tale, pretending with little success that it's for dramatic effect. I am heaving but catch my breath enough to continue as the path ahead flattens.

"I swing round house punches at the guy who shoved me, who backs up into Billy, who shoves the guy forward back at me, right into my fists, one left, one right. I holler like hell 'cause my hands were on fire and I thought broken or whatever, and the guy just goes down. Billy starts laughing and number three comes out of the stall. I'm closer at this point and I shove him back into the stall and he lands flat on his ass wedged between the divider and the toilet. I pick up the tank lid and raise it over my head and the toilet guy shouts, 'No!'"

Arlo gasped, "You didn't."

"I didn't. Billy is kicking the first guy, who fell with great disgrace, and the second guy who connected with my wild hands is still out at our feet. I drop the tank lid away from the bodies and it breaks into three neat pieces but sounded like a 500 pounder. Billy and I stare at each other, bolt out of the head and fly down the stairs. Marco is there and he tells us to keep moving, that he's got it. The rest of the night is kind of blurry." My breathing was ragged and the sentences came out in gasps.

Arlo wanted more. "What about the bar?"

I knew he was breaking my chops and liked my struggling to breathe. "We gave Susan $150 bucks to give to her dad and promised never to come back. But our peers did!"

Billy threw in, too. "Marco was very happy to report that the Navy guys didn't show their faces again, at least during the months we were in Quantico."

I continued. "The next day my right hand is swollen and I can't close it, having broken a small bone on the edge of my fist. No cast, but a splint for a couple weeks, and, yes, at this point I am in trouble with our training officers.

"Billy figures that a simple fight would be just as bad as an avoidable accident, so he develops a story where I kick three Navy asses. Marco is dragged into it, and they both swear to it. I went from being the TBS geek to the Stud Duck. To add color that didn't need it, Marco said that the Navy boys were banished from the bar."

"They bought it?" Arlo was grunting approval.

"The brass bought it. I played the story that I was too drunk to remember much and Billy and Marco kept the yarn straight: all three squids on the deck with me raising the toilet tank lid over my head when my pals burst in on the ruckus. Aside from a little "attaboy" counseling, watch your drinking stuff, nothing ever came of it. But my rep was made forever because my friends lied for me." I wanted to laugh out loud, even now almost 30 years later, but I could not breathe.

Billy poked his finger at both Arlo and me. "If we can't lie for you, why have friends?"

@@@@@

A community event, and all the area recruiters show up.

All of 'em, Army, Navy, Air Force in fatigues, playing with the kids.

Marines are in dress blues, and the kids challenge all of 'em to touch football.

Of course they play, the Marines and Navy team up, and it turns into a tackle game.

A couple busted noses and fingers and a collarbone for the guys in fatigues.

Marines weren't invited back the next year.

@@@@@

We took turns talking about touchy feelie stuff, Billy's first marriage, "doomed from the start," my failure with Judith, "I'm not worthy," and Arlo lamenting the drama of relationships but that he was "willing to take them all out for a test ride."

Billy said that if we wanted female company we wouldn't be taking the Crooked Hooker this weekend.

I took the bait and agreed with him.

"Clem, I would much rather be in the arms of a beautiful woman today, and so would you."

Arlo was enjoying the banter and especially Billy's stories, his pace and candor. "What drives you, Billy?"

Billy seemed caught off guard by the question, just for a beat, and looked up at the cloudy day for inspiration. "Family and friends, I guess. My work. All of it. Being alive." He spread his arms wide.

"Making money, for me." I amaze myself by saying the wrong thing at the wrong time.

Billy shot back right away. "That's sad, Clem. It's why you're miserable."

Arlo interrupted, perhaps to save me from trying to qualify a shallow answer. "Proving my worth, that I am a substantial man in my own right. I am a professional, first and always."

Billy, now in the lead, turned and faced us, he walking backwards, as confident as ever. He commanded our undivided attention.

"You know, people say we signed a check with our lives by joining the military, but that wasn't it for me. I see it all as a matter of faith. Jesus changed the world by dying for everyone, *even His enemies*, the people who crucified him. Not just the turn your cheek, do unto others' stuff. It was revolutionary. And us, the USA, we really are the last best chance on earth for mankind. Arlo, you nearly died to protect people, the Afghans, who, face it, hated you."

Arlo didn't look up and his stride lengthened. "I saw great people die."

Billy was animated but even. "Who died for people who hate you. That's what Jesus did and it changed the world."

I had never heard Billy wax long on religion and I was parts impressed and dismissive. There was not much room for thoughts of the hereafter when I was the center of my universe, from my Audi to my Rolex.

"Well, God knows me," I said to myself.

Billy started to turn as the grade became uneven but managed to say, only to me, "That's a problem, friend. He loves you, but He may not like you."

Arlo heard it and rejoined, "Yeah, but isn't the message about love? Why bust Clem's balls?"

Billy's back was to us now, but he cadenced over his shoulder, "The New Testament is about loving your neighbor as yourself and lots of beautiful stories that are historically corroborated fact. But,

Revelation isn't about love, boys, it's about God's judgment. You gotta be ready because we know not the hour of our end. You gotta be ready!" I could hear his confidence in the timber of his voice.

Arlo looked over his shoulder at me, and I discerned a slight eye roll. "Are you ready, Clem?"

"Probably not."

Billy heard me. "Gotta be ready."

@@@@@

Billy liked when I huffed and puffed. "Hey, Clem, tell the army guy how you got your Bronze Star."

I hated this and Billy knew it.

"Well, Arlo, I got a Bronze Star for driving the regimental commander to a battalion CP."

Arlo looked quizzically at us both. "I thought that was an army thing!"

"Our battalion was the tip of the spear advancing into Kuwait, right at the beginning, February of '91. I was the assistant MMO, maintenance management officer, charged with making sure our supply side Marines stayed out of trouble. They didn't want any and were happy to count canteens and ammo crates. But the battalion had been there for a couple months and everybody was getting antsy.

"For some reason the regimental CO, an older full bird on the list for a brigadier's star, stayed close to our battalion's S-4, the supply guy, my boss. Personalities count, and he, the colonel, didn't like our battalion CO, who everybody loved and respected. I was lukewarm toward all senior field and flag grades, mostly because I was a skinny necked geek... well, I didn't fit the physical profile then, and uh, less so now."

Arlo had the good grace and judgment not to agree. Billy never let me feel inferior because I was not a poster Marine officer, and it secured my loyalty to him. As an adult in my 50's I often lacked the good sense not to make too much fun of my pear-like physique.

"I found myself seated next to Colonel Hardcase in a fast night convoy to catch up to the forward element, and two Marines heard, or thought they heard, small arms fire. I heard nothing. But the colonel radios us to stop, set up a perimeter, and be prepared to engage the enemy, who, if they were there, would have been missed by the battalion CO and would have delighted the colonel."

The boys stopped, thankfully, because I was coughing and slurring my words incoherently.

All Arlo could say was "And?" and Billy cocked his head at me in a *"wait-til-you-hear-this"* look.

I took a big gulp of mountain air. "Now we're stopped. I swear to God, I heard people talking real close to us, in Arabic. Couldn't understand a word, but the colonel was right next to me, on the ground, so I said to him, *"Hear that, sir?"*

"He jumped up like I put a spider on his neck. I took a knee, pistol not yet drawn. *"Where?"* he spat out.

"I started to say, but my voice caught, and all I could do was growl, *"Drop your weapons, surrender!"*

"The colonel knew they didn't hear me, so he shouts in broken Arabic, probably ordering a falafel, really butchers it, and from the darkness these poor slobs start crying and screaming and before you know it a dozen of 'em surrender to the us!

"And they walk right up to the colonel. They're filthy, crying, and looked like they were malnourished and dehydrated. The colonel bulldogs one of them, and another falls on his face."

"That is so cool!" Arlo was excited. "Can I finish it for you?"

I nodded, hard, several times. I was gassed and my feet were on molten rock.

"Colonel, right? Probably post-Vietnam, or never was in-country. Not much on his chest or to show for his rank. Needs a medal, but to get one he needs another hero. You." Arlo beamed.

Billy finished. "Yeah, ego always has something to do with it. Colonel was connected and got a Silver Star for halting the advance of the enemy and getting them to surrender, and Clem took a Bronze Star without the Vee. Everybody won." He punched my shoulder.

"Those Iraqis did, too," I finished. "They had been armed and were sent to harass any movement in that space. They got there late. I never saw so many poor slobs so happy to become prisoner."

Billy called a break and I chugged the last of my water.

"I have more water, Clem, no sweat. I think we only have another hour."

@@@@@

An older civilian on the plane was a real jerk. Pushing the seat in front of him, leaning back and forth, trying to break the thing.

He jumps up when the plane lands, before the "ding."

He's in such a hurry, he yanks open the overhead bin.

He grabs his bag, but another one falls out and hits him in the face.

He drops hard, glasses fall off, his toupee flops open...

Another bag, a bigger one, hits him in the back of the head and he spits his dentures out!

@@@@@

I knew Billy was getting bored with just jawing and telling stories that amused yet did not compel. I was, too, but as long as I was listening while going uphill I just concentrated on steady breathing. It would have been nice to just listen to nothing at all.

Billy filled the void as if talking to himself. "I was out of the Corps for about five years, most of that was spent getting two more degrees, one in public ed and another in Kinesiology."

I cut him off, and gasped at Arlo, "Phys Ed and exercise."

"I know what it is, Clem," Arlo shot back, looking at me like I was a large sweaty rodent.

Billy continued. "Anyway, I was taking every job at the high school I could, in addition to the Algebra and math classes assigned. I was on track to be the head football coach, the job I worked and lobbied for, and coveted. Pride. At the time I was the offensive coordinator and we had much success in our bracket despite average talent and the usual injuries. I was a lock for the job," he grimaced and shook his head widely. "I took a driver's ed segment, my first semester doing so. I was as nervous as the kids and I think it showed and that was a huge negative. The short of it is that I had two cocky kids, a boy and a girl, in the car.

135

"She was driving. He kept harping to crank up the radio. I hadn't controlled the giddiness much up to that point, and I blew my stack at him. Yeah, she hit the brakes for no reason except... me. We get rear-ended, hard, by a tailgater in the middle of the day a quarter mile from the school.

"Airbags, sure, but he was in the back and his seatbelt wasn't fastened. His name was Teddy, well, Teddy shot forward, hit his head funny. Dead."

"Jeez, man. So sorry. Awful," was what Arlo offered. He was stunned.

"Awful doesn't describe it. The investigation exonerated me, but not the school. The girl stuck to the truth, that Teddy was told to buckle and didn't, but I was done. I considered relocating, but the school board insisted I stay, that although I was lucky to stay on the job there would always be a place for me. Parents were supportive. Only one teacher was crazy-hate about me staying in the system. A guy named Lindstrom, a real overly ambitious type I feel sorry for. But bigger things were not gonna come my way."

I said, "Been a while, my friend."

Billy stopped, and we almost crashed into his back. He turned to me, "Clem, that school, that job, those kids and all I do there, and have done there for over 20 years, has been my penance. I think about that kid Teddy every day. I'll die in that job."

@@@@@

Billy took some of my pack, then. I offered him five bucks, and he yelped a small laugh. I underestimated how tough the terrain would be on my knees, shins, and back. I was slowing the expedition down, and with each step it got worse.

Arlo said he could smell rain coming, and I asked him if he really did, and he could only shake his head. Billy was enjoying it all. The conversation had been cloying and intense and his joke lightened the overall mood.

All I smelled was decay, the summer foliage and fallen leaves swiftly dying, the trudge of autumn marching inexorably to winter's death. There was little green left at our elevation but instead of wild colors it looked black and dark and foreboding.

Billy asked, "I wonder what all the critters up here eat, besides some of our garbage?"

"Each other," Arlo said flatly.

@@@@@

We were alone at the top.

The air was thickening when we arrived at the communal campsite in mid-afternoon, sooner than expected, and my back and legs ached in relief. Arlo and Billy were much too chipper for me, and Arlo launched into his best Patton routine when I shrugged off my pack and sat and started chugging water.

"Before we relax, we gotta set up camp. It's gonna rain like crazy and I'm not getting wet if I can help it. Priorities of work, Marine," Arlo said to me, with an arched brow.

Billy was already kicking forest debris from one of the board platforms for a large tent. They were unique to the site and looked like a big pallet: 4x4s about 12 feet long with half inch board, six on top and bottom. The four corners of the platform were

anchored by rebar, good and deep. Six total sleep
platforms sat in a loose circle about 20 feet apart
from each other, with a fire pit in the center that
was charred and well used. If the site was a clock
face, there was an old-fashioned well pump at about
12 o'clock and porta potties were at six. There were
two shallow gullies that I suspected were natural
water run-offs cutting from three to nine o'clock. An
ample supply of cut wood was next to the porta potties, courtesy of Boys Scouts and other volunteers,
who pitched in for projects large and small.

The platform Billy chose was at 9 o'clock. I liked
this one because the thick wooded area was at the
other three ends. Our platform had a ravine or cul-
vert or cliff about 50 feet away and two large trees
with low branches that served as a community
clothesline.

"What will you have me do, right now." I
announced. It was not a question, directed at them
both. It was hard to conceal my fatigue and disgust
at having to get busy right away. The esprit de corps
of the hike up the Broken Femur had evaporated,
at least for me.

Billy spread his arms and commanded with good
humor. "Help Arlo build the tent. Looks like the
Scouts left us plenty of cut wood. I can rig a canopy
that'll allow us a fire if it rains, something small by
our hooch."

I grunted and acted as helper to Arlo's instructions. A smooth operation and we were up and
secure from a frontal assault in ten minutes. It was
a big lightweight state-of-the-art tent, could have
slept four easy, and it had a little entrance for our
packs and shoes. Billy strung up two tarps at hard
offset angles using an adjacent tree and scuffed

out a pit for a small fire. If the rain came straight down we'd be okay, but a deluge or scattered winds would make life miserable. I thought of the girl in the diner in the Ugg Boots. It would have been a long night for her.

I took the initiative to fill our canteens. I then scouted and noted the latrine, and it was good and ripe. I had thoughts of avoiding it entirely and noticed droppings that were not human. I wondered about that but did not voice a concern, and then I stepped in a big pile of crap that was clearly human.

I howled in anger, and though the guys were at least thirty yards away I could hear their muted laughter.

I mumbled to myself wondering why anyone would take a dump out in the open, when Arlo offered while walking toward me, "Maybe because the latrine is in bad shape."

"Well, that SOB did this maybe a day ago, and I have a mind to chase his ass down and..." I was hot as a pistol digging crap from the contours of my walking shoe with a stick.

Billy approached genially, "Clem, you're not running anyone down today. We all need our rest and I'm having hot chow tonight."

"If I keep this boot outside in the rain for a month it's still gonna smell like crap."

As the sun sank to the earth we knew we had the prime location and it would be our own, as no one came up the hill this far today. Most hikers and campers were excellent at self-policing, the random walk path pooper notwithstanding. I had some great memories of spontaneous parties on this hill, all with Judith, and as Billy started cooking and Arlo offered unnecessary advice, I wondered where she was and if she was thinking about me just now.

Arlo kept calling Billy "Billy," as almost no one did but a select few, in my mind. I should not have let it get to me, but on this hike I thought Arlo should be a little less familiar and show Billy more respect, and call him "Coach." I tried to bury the idea that I just did not like Arlo.

Arlo was a real hero. He had earned everyone's, including my, respect for a lifetime. His amused countenance with me was thinly veiled contempt, and I was too old to challenge him and try to earn his respect back. So I pouted.

Billy's cooking snapped me out of my funk. "Aha!" He exclaimed.

"Smells good, Coach," I offered.

Arlo threw in, "It does, Billy! Hey, is that Dinty Moore Stew?"

Billy was pleased. "It is! And I got hot sauce and you better eat it. I've lugged these cans all day!"

I had to smile when he handed me the stew. "Hot sauce, huh? Wonder if I'm gonna leave a surprise for someone tomorrow."

A distant peal of thunder cut off our amusement.

"Maybe it'll skirt us, bounce around and across the hills," said Arlo.

Billy countered, "Or settle on top of this hill."

A light misty rain started, the edge of a terrible storm.

We couldn't make the fire high and brilliant but the offsetting dual lean-to's were doing the job. No wind helped, though at one point we had to hustle to direct the rain away from us.

"Man, that slope is close. Maybe somebody should put up a storm fence, or snow fence there," Billy pointed into the darkness, the firelight reflecting off adjacent bushes, beckoning to an inky wet void.

"Great," I told him. "Let's make sure the water runoff goes right to it." I wasn't much help in the setup process, but commenting was free.

"Well, we'll just report it when we get back," Arlo grunted. "Gonna be real messy tomorrow."

We sat, we drank, we played with the fire, husbanding the dry wood. The rained drummed a little and misted more. We were dry and the fire was hot and not too smoky. We kept it small; rather, Arlo took charge and kept it small, his Smith & Wesson revolver still strapped across his chest.

@@@@@

Billy pulled on the flask. "Arlo, seriously, and no disrespect, but at this point, don't you trust us?"

My neighbor Game told me once when I uttered basically the same thing that when you say "with all due respect" you were going to say something disrespectful. Arlo cocked his head back.

"It's not that, Coach. You're, we're, veterans. Same tribe. We give each other status."

I stretched. "With minorities who are veterans?"

"No." Arlo was flat and adamant. "Just with me. There's still plenty of bias, even racism, in the service."

Billy lurched. "Wait, bias, okay. Everyone has biases. You do."

Arlo spat in the fire. "Sure, but racism in the military is not overt. It's a reflection of the whole country. But it's there. You can't help it, neither can I."

Billy pressed, "Us, meaning white people in general?"

"Well, yeah. Not all, but the ingrained kind that makes assumptions. Not all bad, you know, but not all right, either."

I had to say it. "You mean like we assume army guys are wimps?"

Arlo laughed at that, a standard ribbing we all endure in the tribe.

Billy would not shift to humor just yet. "Arlo, you don't trust any white people, do you?"

"Oh, man, it's not that simple."

Billy said lightly, "Try us."

"I will if you share that flask, Billy," Arlo smiled, and Billy handed it first to me, in turn; I took a pull, and gave it to Arlo who gave me a "not cool" look.

"It's simple. No black people, people of color, will ever trust white. Probably never," Arlo paused to breathe and I took the bait.

"You know, I go out of my way to trust all people of color, maybe to a fault," I whined.

Billy shot out, "Me, too."

Arlo put his arms out using the flask like a shield. "I get it, guys. You must trust people of color or you're a closet racist. I didn't say it's fair to you. We will never completely trust you, though. That's it."

I didn't know how to take that. "How am I supposed to take that?" I tried to sound intelligent. Arlo handed me the flask.

He grinned and shrugged. "It doesn't matter how you take it. You wanted to talk about it. This is talking." The pause was interrupted by distant thunder and thicker air.

Arlo had our attention. "I don't think you all are racists. I do believe in the military community, you know?"

I was still offended. "I'm not a racist, Arlo."

He shook his head, not dismissively, but not on equal ground. "If you have to say it, Clem, then you're not living it."

"What do you mean?" Billy was squinting in the darkness, maybe from unseen smoke.

Arlo stabbed a finger at a point over our heads. "Look, if you're wearing a white hood, you're easy to spot from a mile away. But no one is stupid enough to do that today. If you just live your life I have to judge you based on your actions. But if you say and insist that I'm-not-a-racist you might be protesting too much."

I couldn't let it go. "But I'm not!"

Arlo's grin was genuine. "Easy, Clem. We're cool."

Billy said, under his breath, "I won't be a racist."

Arlo's command posture softened at that admission. "Yeah, Coach, that's it. That's it. You don't just use words, man. You have to live it. Applies to all of us, all colors."

I was still torqued and told them I had black friends.

Billy was disappointed at that. "Oh, for crying out loud, Clem, you sound like a Republican."

Arlo guffawed twice, mockingly. "Okay, I'll play, like who?"

I looked around as if the trees and night sky could bail me out of the hole I had dug.

"Fat Tick. We're tight."

Billy was unimpressed. "That's no endorsement, Clem."

Arlo was amused but loud in his response. "Man, you're ignorant or presumptive or something."

I wasn't going to take too much from this kid half my age, hero or not. "Hey, you can't say anything against my boy!" I bent over, not believing I said that and unable to take it back.

"Oh, he's your boy now. I can't believe you just said that." Arlo squared his shoulders.

My stupid reference went right past Billy. He shot, "Fat Tick is not a good example of a friend, Clem. You're reaching. He's a criminal and you're one encounter away from jail with him around."

Arlo turned abruptly, to Billy. "Why?"

Billy expected support and lost some of his confidence. "Well, he's, you know, a low-level gangster."

Arlo was slowly shaking his head. "He's no criminal, Coach, and he isn't black, either."

Billy and I said in unison, "What?"

Arlo splayed his hands in front of him, speaking slowly as if we were children. "He's Italian. Tiggiero. Anthony Tiggiero."

"You gotta be kidding me," a statement from me, not a question. He wasn't kidding.

"He's still a criminal," Billy said.

It was my turn to enlighten Billy. "The joke's on both of us. I just found out he's an accountant for the *Old Timers*. Big time wheeler dealer."

"Wait a minute..." Billy whipped his head back and forth.

Arlo cut us both off. "You guys think you know so much. Your legs must hurt from jumping to conclusions. Coach thinks Fat Tick is a gangster, and you think he's black. Man, you guys are real stupid for smart white folks."

He said "white folks" as a pejorative, with real derision, dismissing us both on the subject. We sat in silence, passing the booze around.

Arlo wasn't finished. "Oh, yeah, he doesn't drink, either. He spreads money around town, great tipper.

144

Think about the places you been with him, Clem. Ever see a bottle pour for him? Never. He brings business, a buzz, everywhere he goes, real generous with the help, and they'll make sure you and a hundred people stay goofy and stupid and puking and he'll be steady all night."

"How do you know Fat Tick?" I wanted to get away from the race talk.

"No, no, no, what about all your black friends?" He smiled.

"Arlo, I don't know what to say..." I drifted off into a mumble, no help coming from Billy.

Arlo waved a hand. "I get it, Clem. I'm your friend."

"Hear Hear!" Billy exclaimed, and we exchanged glances, and I was relieved. "But how do you..."

Arlo looked at the fire quizzically. "I went out with his crew one night, friend of a friend asked me, but I had a cold and held back. For some reason Fat Tick never wanted me back even though I have had a couple of my boys working on it. Never again because Fat Tick knew what I knew. He's a teetotaler. Shoot, the cops make a show, too, but they get along because when Fat Tick is around, things are chill. Loud, but chill." Arlo had adroitly changed the conversation, for our benefit.

I was still absorbing the accountant revelation from a week ago. I kept close my counsel. Fat Tick had a bad side, very bad. And I was complicit.

"For an Army guy you have real wisdom, Arlo." Billy stood, stretched, and shook his arms. "I'm getting a headache. A real bruiser. Should have drank more water today." He waved off the flask I offered.

I had to say it, and soon. "Gentlemen, I may have to turn back in the morning. These blisters are bad and my right knee is swollen." The night was silent, and the boys didn't help me.

Billy snarled, half-kidding. "Suck it up, Buttercup. You gotta earn this." I tried to protest and he cut me off. "We don't have to decide now, Clem. Clean up your feet some more and we'll see in the morning."

Arlo reached for the flask. "God may decide for us. It's gonna rain like hell."

My brain was swirling from the booze and the dehydration and the aches and pains of the hike, yet my thoughts were lucid. I never saw myself as anything but a regular guy who took people on the merits, though I started with a boatload of presumptions and many were just disgraceful. What should have been a form of redemption for me, being associated with *HHH*, was turning into an emotional and physical disaster. I really wasn't up for this on many levels.

I saw more than suspicion or disgust in Arlo's eyes, in his posture toward me. I saw pity.

@@@@@

Arlo and I started a second short flask. Billy begged off, his brow creased and thick.

Arlo took off his prosthetic and began rubbing his leg. We tried not to stare but Arlo, used to the looks, acted in a matter of fact fashion that eased our awkwardness.

"Hey, uh, what's it like." It came out as a statement, not a question.

Arlo smiled and worked his leg, rubbing and squeezing. "Oh, it's more a nuisance than anything. But I think more about all of it, training, fighting, sacrifice, and death. The higher order, right?"

He had our attention. "God, right, I get it," said Billy.

"Yes, but the whole force of life He provides." Arlo heaved a massive sigh.

I asked, "What's it really like?" Everyone who hasn't been in a firefight wants to know, has to know. I had no embarrassment asking, even though Billy visibly bristled.

Arlo continued and I swear the air moved around him, enveloping his presence. "It's like we're safe on land. Then we're thrown into that ocean of war fighting. Just trying to obey and survive and help the man to your left and your right. Most survive.

"And some thrive, and a very few get churned up, torn apart completely or lost at sea or rescue comes and they throw body parts on the pier. These pieces, these limbs, don't reassemble on their own. They try to knit together but can't. They need help. Some limbs are never found. Here," he pointed to his head, "or here," now slapping his chest.

He pushed on. "Some get thrown back into the ocean when they aren't ready. But the man who went into the sea is not the same as the soldier who came out. There is no peace in this ocean of war. It is constantly moving, churning, pounding itself and everything in it. Salt burns, and then heals. Sand coarsens and then smooths, and in the depths of shadow lurk creatures that indiscriminately feed on smaller, weaker, prey. You're lucky to get out, even if in pieces. But if you don't mend, quickly, you'll rot in the sun and beg to crawl back into the cold deep sea."

We stared for long moments into the fire as it cooled. I stood and placed a couple pieces of wood on the coals, looking at Arlo for approval that I was doing it his way. Billy had his head in his hands.

"Another thought, gents," growled Arlo. "This sea, sea of combat. I was just trying not to drown in all the contradictions and rules of engagement and hating people we don't know and try to protect 'cause... we couldn't trust them all. It was hard to know who to believe, you know?" He threw an imaginary stick at the fire. "I understand what you meant earlier, Coach, I think I do. Loving the people who hate you."

"It's the hardest, and best, thing we can ever do," Billy managed through his hands. "The sacrifice of loving the people who hate you. And it's part of being the professional soldier you are."

"Yeah. I know. I'm swimming hard all the time."

@@@@@

Arlo adjusted his seat, as the smoke, unseen, was getting in his eyes. "Why did you get out of the corps, Coach? Seems to me the Marines would have had to be invented for you."

Billy let out a long sigh. "I did it to myself. We were in Kuwait, mustering to advance into Iraq. I was a rifle platoon commander, had a great platoon sergeant, and all were motivated Marines. We were going to war and we were on top of the world.

"We were quick marching through a crappy area. A civilian, a Kuwaiti, was a few feet away from our approach and in my line of sight. He smacked a woman, an older lady, hard in the face. Knocked her down. She hit the deck and I forearmed him and he landed on his ass. Found out he was her husband.

"He was the HMFIC, of course, of that crappy corner of that crappy village of that crappy country. High offense on my part. By the time we stopped for water ten minutes later I was relieved of my first and only command. I spent the next six months as an assistant S-1 admin at battalion, and it could have been worse. I was a glorified typist, but lucky not to get court-martialed. No hope for a career, and after a few months of that hell I couldn't wait to get out."

I let out an audible "woof." My heart went out to the guy. I considered easing it by throwing myself on the fire of our discussion.

So I did. I recounted the time with Scott Spaeth and the whole story of how I never gave credit to my then good friend of his possible legacy as a co-inventor of the T-Cup. Told it straight, without embellishment or opinion or speculation.

Billy broke the long silence. "You screwed a guy out of his memory."

I didn't ask why he said that, because I knew. "Yeah."

"So, his son, his widow, all they have is the rep of him being a drug freak. Not a co-inventor of a product used by the whole world. Some legacy." His look of disgust was deafening.

I tried to rationalize. "Yeah, but it was only a diagram. I did it, developed it..."

Billy stood. "Some legacy. For both of you. You, you, bastard." He stared at me a long time. If I had moved, he would have decked me. "I have stood up for you, stuck with you, even when you've been nothing but a complete jerk to everyone. I've been tied at the hip with you at the expense of that poor widow and his baby son. It has gotten worse than just being old, and now I see myself more in you than ever, and I don't like it. I am better than this, better than you." He was gasping and spitting and inhaled deeply. "I'm turning in. Tired. Of you, mostly, Clem. If you can hack the rest of this trip, great. But I'm done with your nonsense."

He moved slowly and edged into the darkness toward the tent.

Arlo called out, "Do we get Taps before lights out?"

I heard Billy stop and dreaded the thought he might come back and wear me out again. Arlo had kicked the hornets' nest, but I could not see Billy at this point and I perceived his reflection in the licks and embers of the low fire, a man who trusted and now lost one last strand of faith in a friend.

"No," said Billy. "No Taps tonight."

Arlo spat into the fire and half-whispered, "Let's stay here for a while. Want another pull?" He reached out the flask in my direction without looking at me, keeping his gaze on Billy's receding form in the dark. I took the flask.

"Hey Clem, if there's any pain in emotional conflict, your man Coach B is in agony."

I waited until I heard Billy enter the tent. I assumed he would cool off, but his condemnation sounded final. I should never have told him, but I thought I could ease some of the pain he felt. I only made it worse. "Arlo, I have to tell you something. About Fat Tick."

Arlo said low, "Man, you're obsessing, really. Let it go."

I was half lit and needed to be heard, needed reassurance. "I couldn't tell Billy. It would justify his hate of the guy."

He raised his eyebrows. Even heroes like a little gossip.

As conspiratorially as I could without slurring my words, "Remember the Silver Spur fight? About four years ago?"

"Yeah." In a second recognition widened his eyes. "No!"

I had his attention and I made the most of it. "Oh, yeah. Crazy night out with Fat Tick. I staggered out the back of the Spur having already puked on myself. Four guys came up right behind me, into the alley we go, them yelling that I disrespected their women or horses or I don't know what. I took a hard shot to the head. Next thing I remember is Fat Tick is picking me up, trying to get me to stand, stopping my head from bleeding, begging me to be okay. I saw four guys on the ground." With each word Arlo leaned closer and ducked his head as his eyes got impossibly wide.

"Holy crap. Holy, holy crap. Two guys were almost blinded, man. One lost all his teeth and a big chunk of his tongue. The fourth guy..." Arlo was speaking to himself.

I finished his sentence. "He didn't wake up for two months and still drools on himself."

We sat in quiet for a few minutes, listening to the silence before a storm. Leaves rustled, but no other emanations of nature except the crackling of the fire.

I filled the void. "Fat Tick was worked up. Told me he thought they killed me. Another dude rolls up in a car. Big guy. He had big ass rings on his hands, both hands covered in bloo... oh my God!" I stood quickly.

Arlo whipped his head around, staring into the darkness. "What?"

"The guy who drove us out of there. It was Boo-Boo. I remember his hands, now, they were huge, almost as big as Fat Tick's. His rings!"

Arlo told me to sit down, now.

"I have tried to bury that, Arlo. Never told a soul."

"Clem."

"Jeez, Arlo, I, I never saw what happened."

Arlo was hard and commanding. "Pay real close attention, Clem. Forget you told me anything. Forget you remember anything. Keep Boo out of your thoughts on this."

"Man, what am I going to do?"

"You're going to do nothing. Nothing. Fat Tick may have saved your life. And those shit kickers got more than what they deserved, but that doesn't matter today. You saw nothing. You remember nothing. Bury it."

"He saved my ass twice. Damn."

"Clem, he owes you, too. Whoa. I heard Fat Tick had a temper, but whoa. You breathe a word of this, ever again, you might find out just how dark his other side really is."

I exhaled long and loud. "Billy was right."

"Yeah."

An hour later we entered the tent having drunk too much, the second flask nearly empty. Telling tall tales and whoppers has a way of doing that. Billy was already asleep, in the center, his head away from both of ours. Arlo and I hit the sack in silence, he removing his prosthetic and rubbing the stump, and me trying not to stare at him trying to ignore me.

Then the rain came.

18

NOVEMBER 1

The wind and rain beat a steady tattoo on our tent, buffeting in all directions at once as if we were the apogee of the storm. I slept fitfully, waking at odd hours, checking my watch at odd intervals. I tried to will myself to sleep, but the storm had other plans. I cursed at the wedge I drove between Billy and me, an unnecessary mistake of judgment, the story of my life. Arlo slept, snoring without a care throughout it all. I heard Billy give a loud start sometime after midnight. I faced away from him and Arlo, only looking over once or twice; Billy was on his back, and Arlo faced his side of the tent. The intermittent lightning was sharp and I counted the one thousand two thousand, many times, calculating the distance from the flash of light with the following thunderclaps. Although the lightning stayed two-plus miles away the downpour made clear we were in the heart of the storm.

At 0256 precisely, according to my trusty Rolex, the lightning and thunder and rain rolled over each other, the storm right above us, the water running just underneath the wooden platform, and I thought we might be swept away, and if not for my aching body and abject fatigue I would have bolted right then and there. Just as sudden the flashes of lightning and concussive peals of thunder stopped while the rain beat the tent and I drifted off to a dreamless slumber.

@@@@@

"*Jeez*, Clem. *Clem!*"

Arlo was calling me, loud, trying to be heard over a new steady drumbeat of rain. I was barely conscious, my legs and back and feet on fire and I had to take a leak, my first thoughts. My bones ached so much I considered just going in the tent. It was 0655.

"*He's dead!*" Arlo almost shrieked, his flashlight in hand shone on Billy's face.

I tried and failed to pop out of the sleeping bag, wrestling with the zipper and almost falling into the side of the tent, which might have toppled it. A flash of hard rain soaked the whole skin of it, the wind howling.

"What, *what*? Are you sure?"

"I'm sure, man." He exhaled loudly. "Dead for hours."

"Check for a pulse, Arlo, we can revive him..."

He kept the light on Billy's face. "I know a dead man when I see one. I already checked his pulse." Arlo was very close to Billy's face, inches away, the light trained on the visage. Billy's eyes were wide open, mouth crooked and agape, slack, and his jaw was off-center.

I was horrified. Billy looked very dead. I flew into a panicked rage.

"What the hell did you do, Arlo?" I screamed at him stupidly. "Why didn't you wake me earlier? Why..." I grabbed his collar, one of many mistakes I would make in the minutes to come.

He dropped the flashlight and we fell into the semi-darkness when his left fist crashed into my jaw, sending me backwards from my kneeling position. I scrambled up to a crouch ready to pounce despite my body protesting in a thousand aches and pains and I threw two punches connecting with only air. I had murder on my mind, first that Arlo killed Billy and intended to kill me, and that I was determined to kill Arlo first.

"You ass." Arlo was calm, but angry. "I'll set this leg on and then I'll beat you silly later." The flashlight was pointed at the back of the tent and his silhouette was clear.

I sprang at him, screaming. His eyes popped in shock as I crashed into his torso and as I grabbed him in a tackle I tumbled over him, my feet flying over my head. My toes skidded lightly on the top of the tent then my knees hit the back of the tent and the wind caught a pocket of air underneath and behind us, the rain sounding like a jet, and the whole hooch became unmoored in as many seconds.

We were now a ball of bodies and tenting and bags and gear, pelted by rain and dropping into the mud, the three of us entangled, gear hitting us freely and I caught Billy's bugle over my left eye and I felt the heat of blood over my face. Arlo shouted to let him go, and I did, the momentum of the tent stopping but still sliding by our inertia, the wet slope, and the incessant rain.

We had tumbled and somersaulted at least twice, and the tent opened at our heads, rain pouring in. We could feel the river of mud we were on, and without a word we scrambled to get out of the tent, the precipice near our bivouac known but unsure of how close we were to tumbling down a rocky and steep decline.

Arlo threw himself out of the opening, and I grabbed Billy and pushed him, bag and all, out to Arlo's grasp, when he gestured behind me with his eyes and head. I turned and saw Arlo's prosthetic a hand away but as I reached to it the shift in weight pulled the tent, now filling with water and me in it, faster to the unknown. Arlo yelled, "Screw it," grasped Billy and threw his bulk in the bag behind him out of the tent, and grabbed my arm, pulling, as I heaved myself out.

We were slipping and sliding in a river of mud, Arlo scrambling to get to the wood platform barely seen about 20 feet away. I dug my toes in to follow him and Billy crashed into me. I clung to my dead friend and the earth beneath me fell away. I had a bear hug on Billy and I panicked, kicking my feet as I tried to stand vertical, my hips and shoulders to the ground, with a waterfall of sludge at my back.

My left foot caught a step, a rock or tree root or something and my momentum stopped. I was disoriented and in the next breath I realized I was standing upright. Mud and water crashed over me, and I instinctively dug Billy's head and shoulders into the face of the cliff for purchase, for safety, for leverage, for the love of God.

No more sliding, but it was slippery and I dared not move out of fear of losing this safe haven. Although blinded by the mud I could picture the drop-off clearly having inspected it yesterday in the daylight. I wondered if Arlo went over the cliff. I wondered if it was inevitable for me.

"Clem!" Arlo, above me, shouting out over my head, shouting to the bottom of the crevasse. I could not answer or see, mud was in my eyes and nose and mouth and I spat and gagged and coughed.

"Clem!"

The rain abated and the river of mud slowed but still moved.

"Yeah," I croaked, and louder, "Right here."

"I can't see you, man." He sounded both agonized and relieved. "Can you climb back up here?"

I thought for a second, my breath coming out in coughs. "No." Billy was still in his sleeping sack, both of us covered in mud, and my bearhug was the only thing I was sure I could control.

"What? What? Something wrong? Broke something? What?" Arlo was intense and serious.

"I have Billy."

The mud stopped sliding and the wind picked up from the bottom of the crevasse and blew in my face. I could hear a stream of curses above me, part annoyance and part problem solving.

"Okay, Clem." He was calming down. "Do you need help? The break in the weather may only be for a couple minutes."

I think I told him I couldn't see, had a precarious foothold and didn't know if I would free fall or just slide to a slow death and I wasn't letting go of Billy. But I didn't.

"I'm not moving, dammit!" I yelled, which came out in a shriek.

"Be cool, man. I think I can get to you now," Arlo said, cold as ice.

I could hear his exertions above me.

"Jeez, Clem. You wanna die? Let him go and you can probably climb up here."

"I still can't see, Arlo."

"Let him go and wipe your eyes!"

I was frightened by my own resolve. "No," I coughed, when in fact I was frozen in fear. I still could not see.

"Dammit," he spat, not a curse but a statement. I could hear Arlo crawling away, keeping up a narrative like he was talking to someone wounded in battle who needed human contact, to take a soldier's scarred body away from thinking too much about his immediate danger.

"I lost the prosthetic when the tent went over. There's that nylon line secured near the platform... here!" He grunted. "Damn knot." Cursing, then a cry of triumph. "Okay I'm gonna anchor this here. I think it's long enough." The words came garbled and gauzy and the faint sounds of the predawn were hollow in the ringing in my ears. Sludge started to harden all around me, my head, ears, eyes, shoulders, and mouth. I clung to Billy as if a life raft although his body would probably bring me down to an unseen bottom. The slightest tension in my grip loosened the foothold my heels had in the still unidentified step that held me up. In my panic I stopped breathing. I spat through the dirt and exhaled a puff of mud, inhaling shallow and long trying to calm myself.

"Clem!" Arlo was above my head, his voice strong and clear in the early morning quiet.

I popped out through pursed lips having swallowed enough mud, "Yeah."

"There's," he paused, lowering his tone, "there's just enough rope. I, I, made a loop, to grab. For you to grab."

"Yeah. No!" I did not know how I was to grab anything as my grip on Billy's midsection tightened.

Curses from above. Arlo could not have been more than a few feet above my head.

"Look, Clem. We're not gonna make it if you hold him. He's gone." His exasperation bordered on desperate. "Let him go. You have to help me here or..."

"Screw off. I'm not letting him go." I sounded tougher than I felt, my resolve loosening my grip on Billy and my foothold in equal measure. I leaned back, Billy's head hitting the mud face of the cliff behind me. My feet slipped an inch and I dug his head in for leverage.

"Don't move, Clem." Rustling, hard breaths. "Hey, I made a loop. It's gonna be close, about a foot over your head. It's the only option. Throw your right hand up and I'll loop this around your wrist," he said, plain and urgent and steady, commanding and paternal. It was hopeless.

I nearly sobbed at the futility and absurdity. I slid another inch, yelping.

"Clem, do it now!"

Still clutching Billy, I thrust my right arm straight up, feeling the caking mud weigh my shoulder. Billy slipped and I tightened my grip on his torso as my feet came free and I felt the coarsened nylon rope whip over my hand and I tried to grab it and I thought it fell away.

The cord tightened aggressively around my wrist as the nylon caught and then cinched in an iron hold. My feet fell free, Billy slid some more, and I pulled in my forearm holding him digging my fingers into a slimy fold of the bag and I bit down hard on his upper arm encased in the muddy synthetic fiber, both to arrest his freefall and scream in pain.

"*Yes!*" exclaimed Arlo in triumph. "You're good, man, you're good!" I heard him crawl away and return. I felt far from good. My wrist seemed severed and my shoulder was on fire.

"Okay, Clem. Last chance here. Something has to give. I can't haul you up, both of you up. I'm not anchored well myself, uh, not well at all."

I grunted through my bite, neither assent nor dissent, hanging by my wrist and nearly swinging from it. I tried to get my feet back on firm ground.

"Look, man, you have to let him go. We'll come back later for him. I promise."

Arlo had lost the timber in his voice. I believed then he was lying to me, the way a corpsman or combat medic has to lie to someone doomed, that he'll be alright just stay awake and how about that time we... At that moment, I thought he would lie to a man who was going to die. He just might. I wasn't ready to die, not by a longshot. I wasn't ready. Not even close.

I lost track of everything but the pain as I teetered on the brink. My wrist and shoulder screamed and all I could do was concentrate on holding Billy.

Arlo's curses above me were hard, violent, and frustrated, oaths against all life and the heavens above.

"Clem. Clem. I can reach only so far. I'll, I'll grab Billy and pull him up but you have to help, push him up higher than where you have him."

In that dark corner of my mind I saw Arlo deliberately dropping my friend. Releasing my bite from Billy's arm, I cried out, "Don't drop him, don't, don't..."

A fresh torrent of curses, and I mused that Billy would have been both shocked and grudgingly impressed. I had never heard some of Arlo's epithets, and their combinations, ever.

I was light-headed and giddy at the absurdity of it all. He caught his monologue and got serious.

"I won't, Clem. You gotta do this now. Your arm will be useless if you hang much longer. Do it now."

I felt the rope tug slightly and realized that Arlo must be using it also for a hold. I had Billy around the high waist and tried to scooch him up a little to better grab him lower on his hips. My right arm, shoulder to wrist, screeched in pain as Billy's head caught and then was free of the wall of packed earth behind me. I kicked my legs and found the step, the one I lost before.

"Wait!" I yelled. "Wait!" My chest heaved as I sucked in air, the taut chord still holding me fast. More confident, I exclaimed, "Okay, now!" as I thrust Billy up and my grip went around his lower hips.

"That's good, that's good, Clem. I've got him!" And Billy was free. I waited for a crash below me but all I heard was Arlo grunting and crawling as I threw my now free hand over the rope on my right. I pulled the cord to accept some of the weight and blood surged back into my shoulder though my hand stayed numb. I started my own stream of expletives.

"Calm down, Clem. I'm coming for you now." I could tell he was now above me. "How about I pull you up by your free hand, okay? Help me by digging your heels up and in."

"When?"

"Now!"

I kicked and dug, raising my left arm until his fingers touched mine and we tightened our fists together in a grasp that was firm but tenuous.

Arlo grunted. "C'mon, man. I need you just a little bit higher."

I raised one leg, bent the knee, and dug the heel into the face of the wall, pushing up and raising myself enough to feel slack on my roped hand and Arlo's free hand to grab my left wrist, still locked up in his other fist. I cried out in relief.

"I got you, Clem, I got you. Try to help me, it's real loose up here now. Your damn watch is in the way."

Two, then three heel steps and Arlo had my upper arm, shoulder, and chest and hips until I tried to sit on the ledge, still blinded by mud, exhausted, pained.

"No, no, keep moving, keep moving." Arlo's urgency was new, and I crab-walked backwards and I felt Arlo go and as I moved back a sharp tug on the rope, new pain mixed with old, listening to Arlo grunt as he pulled me up the slight rise, still unseen.

The rise continued. I gulped air and moved with a deep resolve, instinctively aware of Arlo's distress and knowing that we were not out of danger. I stopped when my right hand, rope tight around my wrist but slack otherwise, hit the wooden platform.

"Jeez, Clem, you're a load."

"I can't see." I couldn't raise my arms, either, but admission was weakness and I still didn't know if Billy was safe and secure and maybe he was still alive and slept through it all.

I leaned back and struggled to control my breathing. Mud drenched my face and using a piece of his shirt Arlo wiped away crud, he talking matter-of-factly in the not-so-soothing tones of a drill

162

instructor. The first thing I saw was his scowl bathed in sweat and grime. And the dawn, clear and cool.

"Where's…"

"Right here, Clem. We're secure."

The sleeping bag with Billy's remains was curled on the platform. I looked to the edge of the precipice and I swear the ground was still moving, oozing to the edge maybe 20 feet away. The day before it was more than twice that. The hilltop looked like a dirt iceberg. All our gear was gone.

"Holy," was all I could say.

"Holy nothing, Marine. That was close."

"How'd you do that, get me?"

"Later. The job's not done. We need to get off this platform. I think it's coming unmoored." He gave the wooden slats a shake with one hand and it appeared to move freely.

I turned to all fours and winced, "My arm. It's effed up real bad. Not broken, but…"

"Clem, you probably ruptured every tendon and ligament on that side. Crawl toward the pump. I'll get Billy."

We crawled forward, up hill, where yesterday it was flat. It was then that I noticed consciously that Arlo was working on one leg, scratching himself forward while hauling Billy's remains. The earth still oozed, slow but steady, and powerful.

"Jeez, Arlo, your leg." The gravity of his effort to save me was overwhelming.

"Yeah. To the pump, Clem. Fifty-meter target. The pump."

We moved steadily but it was difficult. Each hand or knee or toe hold forward invited a slide back. I couldn't offer to help him, even though he only had one leg, I had only one arm. The pump was about twenty meters away and although the ground stopped moving it was slow and sloppy work, and it took several long minutes to cover the ground.

Arlo shook the steel pipe. "Secure, all good, I think." He knelt and pumped the handle, alternating gulps of water and washing his hands and face. "Get your head in there." I did, washing with my left hand as best I could.

As I tried to clear my head of mud in every hole, Arlo shifted on his full leg, crossing his arms as his injured leg stuck into the mud.

"Listen, Clem. Just listen."

I kept washing in futility and nodded.

"We can't stay up here, the exposure could be brutal, weather and whatever. We must make it down the hill. Think, man. We can't take Billy."

I started to protest.

"Save it, Clem. I'll need help walking. We're covered in mud and muck. You're in shock. The sooner we get going the sooner we can get help to recover Billy, later. Tomorrow."

I knew he was right on all counts.

"You done?" I was thinking clearly, shock or not.

Arlo chuckled in a phlegmy rasp. "Yeah, for now, or until you say something stupid." He smiled.

"Thanks. I'm trying to figure out how..." I pointed to the slope, "How you did it." The ground was hardening quickly, brownish red in a slope that would have daunted a skier if it was snow.

"I'm a professional soldier, Clem. I just did what I had to do."

The sun bathed my face and his back. I never loved the sun so much as at that moment.

Arlo started cursing again, a sincere gesture of humility. He sat with crossed legs. We were caked in sludge, exhausted, in pain, and lucky to be alive. Arlo saved my life and Billy's body. I just shook my head, in awe, and we both looked first at his leg, the stump below the knee, then to the mud-caked bag that held Billy's remains.

"We can't go anywhere covered in this," I implored. "I know we have to get moving, but we'll be carrying too much extra weight. Let's wash it all, our clothes, his, his bag, and let the sun and wind dry us out. I think it's warming up."

The quick fury in Arlo's eyes spoke volumes. Without a word he began to take the gun holster off his chest, then his shirt. We stripped and rinsed off and wrung out our clothes in silence.

There wasn't much to do for ourselves. Shirt, socks, trousers. Neither of us had shoes. He handled his weapon gingerly. It was so thick with mud it looked like a football.

"I had to use this," Arlo waved the gun, "As a mountaineer pick. Saved us, ha." He shook it, ejected the six round clip and nodded in resignation.

Now stripped myself, I pumped the well handle and he placed the weapon under the hiccupping stream. "Hope it doesn't rust today. Do you have your 9mm?" His clogged weapon cleared of the thick sludge quickly.

I had not thought of it. "What you see is what I have, Arlo. I think everything went over the cliff." Arlo worked the cylinder action on his gun and set two clips on the hard ground with it.

Arlo sighed. "Can you somehow get our clothes hung up on that tree? Or there?" He pointed at the obvious places. "And pinch your eye wound, at least try to. You'll need a stitch."

I stood shivering as I willed the sun to have the right effect. I began placing articles around nature's clothesline of trees and brush, working to keep it all in the rising sun. Nude, wet, cold to the bone, I began to shake harder, which grew as I realized this was an exercise in futility: our clothes would never dry enough, maybe not all day long; without shoes we couldn't get far; carrying Billy, or dragging him, would be too difficult as my arm was starting to protest while my adrenaline began to fade.

Standing tall for the first time since last night, I could survey the area more. The ground was not yet hard packed. Our platform, normally fifty-plus feet from the ravine, was closer to half that now, and new gullies had formed surrounding it. I marveled at how it happened and tried to follow the origins uphill and could not determine the source of the river of water. My anxiety grew and I quaked harder.

Arlo barked, "We're gonna have to get dressed soon, Clem. Soon. This can't sustain..." He was wrestling with Billy in his bag, which had taken on a lot of water and mud.

I breathed deep, ready to assent to his next words, that we had to leave Billy if we were to survive. Looking directly into the sun I prayed, hard and deep and earnest, from the bottom of my soul. I wanted peace and rest, I wanted Billy alive, Arlo's leg back, Judith to weep for me, and for God to pick me up and take me home. My eyes burned and I looked away from the sun and I spied a backpack clinging to the platform.

I gingerly walked to it, feet squishing into the mud and sucking when they came out, but not enough to cover the top of my bare feet. It was Billy's waterproof pack. I fell on my knees and whooped next to it like a puppy with a new friend.

"What the…" I could hear Arlo trying to get to me.

"Son of a bee!" I stood holding Billy's pack aloft. "We're in business!" It was a miracle it didn't go over the edge and it was still water-tight.

The pack had dry clothes, enough for both of us. An extra pair of sneakers, and many socks, too, and although a size too big I dreamed of lacing the shoes on good and tight. A couple butterflies and a large band-aid to cover my eyebrow wound.

"Let's strip Billy, and clean out the bag," I ordered, "Before we put this stuff on."

Arlo's brief happiness at dry clothes was short-lived. "Clem, c'mon. This is gonna be tough enough." His frustration had returned.

"I'm taking him down the hill, Arlo. Come with us or stay." I stood over him, hands on hips.

"You can't drag us both. You can't carry him alone. If you don't help me, as a three legged-man, I'll have to crawl. Jeez, Clem, you gotta think this through." His eyes were daggers. Arlo had saved my life and I was consigning him to crawling like a beast while I walked in dry shoes tending to a dead man.

I knelt. "I'm not leaving him, Arlo. We must do this. We'll figure it out."

He closed his mouth and gently closed his eyes, breathing deep and slow. When he opened them my mug was a foot from his, a look of resignation, a battle he couldn't win.

"Clem, I promised my mother I would never argue with a naked man on a dirt mountain after almost drowning in mud." His offered a thin smile but his eyes remained dark and unkind.

I nodded in relief and appreciation. We got to work cleaning up Billy and the bag. I was surprised how detached I was, and realized it was the chill and all I wanted was to put my dead friend's clothes and shoes on me.

We agreed through grunts and sighs to wait for an hour or so in order for us to be dry and let the rising sun, clear sky, and wind hard pack the gradient of our route. We spent a long time cleaning Billy and rinsing the sleeping bag, which was completely sodden and if I hadn't mitigated it by wringing the hell out of the bag, it would have added forty pounds however we dragged or carried him.

Arlo speculated on what happened to Billy, a heart attack or an aneurism. "What the heck happened, man." A statement, talking to himself.

I resolved to worry about what was in front of me, a twelve-plus mile hike, mostly downhill, carrying nearly 200 pounds on my shoulders. Arlo had already committed to drag himself. "You take the Coach, Clem. I'll worry about me."

I was ready to go by 0900, and I said I needed five minutes of shut-eye. Arlo thought that was a good idea, so we eased ourselves onto the platform nearest the pump. We left Billy where he was, now encased in the bag. I lay back and closed my eyes.

A crash in the brush startled both of us awake. I jumped up and low-stepped to it, and Arlo laughed.

"Hey, Clem. The storm wreaked havoc on the ecosystem. Rabbits, mostly. I read they haven't seen anything much bigger in years up here."

"I don't know what I thought I would do." I stretched. "Besides, you have the rabbit cannon. I'll be ready to go after a head call." The latrine was beyond use for practical purposes, the bottom of the crappers buried under a foot of hardening sludge. I used the bushes that didn't alarm me, my modesty and decorum long gone. Arlo asked me the time and I told him, trying to sound matter of fact.

Arlo shouted, "Damn! We slept two hours, it's almost eleven? Damn! We gotta move, man, we have a lot of trail to cover at a slow pace." He relieved himself right at the platform.

We discussed each of us using one shoe, but Billy's size was a couple too small for Arlo.

I stared at the sealed bag with Billy's remains. My arm throbbed but I could work it; Arlo had his water cleared revolver loaded across his chest, my one-legged Pancho Villa, with Billy's K-bar (found in his pack) jammed next to the gun, and a sturdy walking stick he foraged for in a flash. I hoisted Billy onto my shoulders in a fireman's carry, using a technique I saw on-line by rolling over him and using my momentum and legs to manage it, and it was surprisingly effective. Arlo was impressed.

"Hey, you made that look easy, Clem. See that one on-line? Army's been doing it for years."

I told him to stuff it, and he scooted on his ass, backwards, taking the lead. I trudged behind him, my shoulder and arm on fire, knowing we were not likely to get very far. Arlo whistled, avoiding my gaze. He risked his life for me, and further serious injury now going blind down the hill so I could feed my ego and guilt by carrying my dead friend. Arlo crawled now because I couldn't see the light, see his way, and I swear he read my mind.

"He was my friend, too, Clem. We do what we should do, all in. I'm just gonna worry about me. You worry about you two. Giddy-up, Marine."

He moved faster than me, but even in the best of passages the going was slow. We didn't talk; at least, I couldn't talk. We stopped frequently, me leaning against a tree or kneeling, and by his attitude I knew he was annoyed, but it couldn't be avoided.

At one point I made a joking reference about an old comedy film, "*Weekend at Bernie's*," scoffing at the absurdity of our situation.

"What are you talking about? Never saw it, man. Save your breath."

That movie, equally stupid and funny, was made before he was born. The gap in our ages was felt in every step I took. I tried to roll my feet, I tried to keep the center of gravity over my hips, I tried to act like more of a man than I was.

At the first rest stop Arlo could barely suppress his fury, crawling into some brush and mumbling that he had to make crutches. "My ass is killing me." I offered to help look for suitable thick sticks and he grunted derisively. We both knew I wasn't going to put Billy on the ground.

The attempt at using crutches lasted less than a hundred yards. The branches were all too wet, slimy, or brittle. Arlo went back to dragging himself.

We heard fauna frequently, sometimes very close. It was a beautiful awful day. Fat clouds moved quickly in the sky as the sun poked out in shifts, giving us warmth when we needed it, and hiding when we were overheated.

We trudged, we slid, we reserved our wind and did not speak on the move. My ankles were bursting, my back screamed, and I held Billy aloft on my shoulder while dangling my damaged arm most of the time.

At the third or fourth rest, Arlo had a small epiphany of sorts that I thought was unimportant.

"You know, now I get it. Why Fat Tick didn't include me again."

I was too exhausted to mumble a response.

"He must be tight with Boo-Boo. And Boo is my second father, who would have kept me away from that potential for extreme violence. And I thought it had to do with me." He looked up as the clouds skittered by on the clear ice of the blue sky.

Hours passed. We took fewer breaks. I don't know how far we went, but Arlo speculated about four miles, maybe one mile an hour, tops. The sun was at a hard angle and the clouds disappeared while a ceiling of grey was pulled across the sky. It got cooler and when mixed with our sweat we were chilled. Arlo was soaked, sliding on his rump all day, using the K-bar as a pick and pulling himself to meet it. He had abandoned the large stick long before, and I could tell the dragging had taken a painful toll on his back and hips, as his every move was accompanied with a curse or gasp or muffled grunt.

Arlo always kept the lead and the pace.

Billy's last words knocked on my skull, my head and heart thundering. He had said he was tired of my nonsense, that he was through with me. My penance was my own fatigue in bearing him now. I wondered if he knew what I was doing and thought he might admonish me for carrying him for my own redemption, not to protect him. I fought back the horror of those last moments when he condemned me. I could never explain my lack of action and he could never take his words back. Billy's last conscious thoughts were despising me when it should have been something beautiful.

I began to daydream about sleep, completely outside of my body. The knifing pain in my neck, legs, arms and back was wild in its proportions, like being hit with hammers in different places at the same time. I whistled by accident when I inhaled, as even my teeth and tongue were ablaze in rips of pain.

A strange crash from the brush behind me. I turned my torso and spied a dirty white-grey big thing, low to the ground, that I first thought was a fat bear. The snout gave it away in the next second: a feral boar, and I screamed in terror.

Arlo was facing to the rear and stopped. I took the few steps to place Arlo between me and the beast. It was thirty feet away and closing fast.

Arlo yanked his gun out of the holster like he did it every day, flipping back the hammer with his thumb and waited one count, and fired. The first round hit the monster in the throat just off center and its momentum hesitated for a heartbeat, but it kept charging us, squealing in fury. Arlo then put five rounds in rapid succession in the same spot, a fist sized group, and the boar's front legs stopped working, its head lolled to the side, its snout and front legs dug into the earth in one last act, back legs still working hard without effect. The grey-white hog collapsed six feet from Arlo's toes.

"*HO!*"

Behind me, more crashing, and a giant of a man in modified Boy Scout gear burst through the brush.

"Holy Moly! That's some great shooting!"

I couldn't keep turning around. Kids were behind the man. All I could say was, "Arlo, put the gun down."

"No need, gentlemen. I counted six." His voice boomed, deep and clear, cutting though the ringing in my ears from the echo of Arlo's revolver. "Uh, you might want to put down, easy, what do you have there." He said to me, his face close to mine.

The man looked up and it was then that I realized I was holding Billy high over my head with every intention of throwing him at the charging, and now very dead, beast.

The Big Boy Scout didn't help me. I lowered Billy to the ground at my feet. It was then I catalogued the scouts, eight or nine of them, ranging in age from young teen to two very official looking older teens, one of whom could probably use a shave.

"I'm Ed Coffey," said the big guy as he strode to the boar carcass. "Holy Moly. That is one big feral pig. Albino, never saw one this close. Maybe 250, 300 pounds. Damn good shooting, too, soldier. Damn good shooting. You saved your," he looked at me quizzically, "Lives. Holy Moly."

Coffey was big across the shoulders straining against a threadbare boy scout uniform shirt, powerful legs encased in cargo shorts, brush cut head with aviator glasses, a massive gaucho style mustache which hid his mouth making his utterances difficult to anticipate. Every word was a clap of thunder, even when conversational.

"Good to meet you, Mr. Coffey. I'm Arlo. Arlo McIlhenny. The pall bearer is Clem Reeger. Long story." Arlo's head twitched and he sighed with relief. I kept one hand possessively on Billy's chest.

"Later, Arlo. I'll want to hear it all. But we have work to do. I expected to be at the end of the Bent Femur by now with my Scouts, but we got a late start. Glad we caught you here."

Coffey started giving orders to the two older scouts now surrounding us in an even keeled fashion, as if ordering camping equipment, with an urgency never far from his eyes that continually scanned the area where the boar came out of the brush. I picked out most of the phrases through the roar in my head, two litters to be built, stay together, don't stray, make plenty of noise. And to move quickly.

"Arlo." Coffey was used to being in charge, confident and alert. "Do you have a reload for that?"

"Yeah, one more ring, I do."

"Load it then, please. Big Momma here was hungry and there might be piglets, and not the cute kind. Mind my scouts." Coffey had a formal way of speaking that was reassuring.

"Yes, sir." Arlo was all business, but in pain. His face was greyed like the sky and that's when I noticed blood pooling underneath him, not a lot, but enough to give me a start. Coffey saw it, too.

"Arlo, you're injured and I want to tend to it," Coffey said evenly, "No time to waste."

The scouts made two litters, harrumphing and chirping in equal parts, as Coffey tended to the backside wounds of Arlo. Coffey glanced often at me, with a look of mixed incredulity and what I took to be reproach. I kept one hand on Billy, trying without success to ignore Coffey's disdain.

Arlo never took his eyes off the beast he killed. "Can you make a third litter?" Only half-kidding.

Coffey dismissed the idea immediately. "Not a chance, too heavy and too dangerous. Pigs will eat anything and we'll need the safe cover the distraction of the carcass will give us." He looked at me and then the body bag.

"Now's the time, Reeger, to tell me about what you're carrying."

I looked him dead in the eye and stayed mute because if I opened my mouth I would have burst into tears, which came anyway.

I felt a small hand on my shoulder, and my tears became gasping sobs. The voice attached to the little hand kept saying, "It's okay, mister, it's okay."

I heard Arlo and Coffey talking in low tones and wanted to contribute, but I couldn't. I looked up at the hand on my shoulder. A round face under a boy scout cap in full uniform regalia, sash and all, unlike the other boys who appeared to be dressed for work and comfort. He kept patting my shoulder, repeating his mantra, "It's okay, mister."

He had Down's Syndrome, I think. I didn't have any experience with those kids, none at all, and I startled him when I recognized his face and manner. He smiled more broadly, keeping up the soft touch in a rhythmic pattern. "It's okay, mister."

I was spent. Every bone ached. Arlo had saved us and all I could do was prepare to throw Billy at the boar, the whole point of taking him with us shattered by my cowardice and fear. If I had not insisted on carrying Billy in the first place, then Arlo would not have scraped his back on the ground, no blood trail, and no boar that would have made quick work of us. Or just Billy. Or just Arlo. I probably would have run. With one heave I tried to control my emotions.

Arlo and Coffey were staring at me, without expression. I could not look at them, so I looked up at my new friend.

"I'm Jimbo. He's," and Jimbo pointed at the tallest scout, "He's Phillip. My older brother. Everyone says we're twins but we're not, he's a year older. He's the coolest guy we know, everyone says so." Jimbo stuck out his hand for a shake.

I moved my hand off Billy's chest and took Jimbo's small soft paw. "I'm Clem. And thanks."

Before we left Coffey had the boys take pictures of the feral pig and Arlo mugged for the camera, the Great Albino-Pig Hunter. It was a light moment for all the boys, all in wonder and awe. They showed their individual and collective chops, too. An impressive group.

We were moving in ten minutes and would have left sooner but they were all giving me a wide berth, men and boys. I was still heaving and sobbing intermittently without shame or care until a few moments before we began down the hill. When I got it together, Coffey directed me to take the right yoke of the front litter, for Billy, with Phillip taking the left. Two mid-sized boys strained at the rear. The second litter was a three-man operation, two big kids taking the front, Coffey alone at the rear, keeping Arlo aloft.

Coffey in charge. "I'm concerned about jostling you too much, Arlo. We'll keep going as long as we can. But we move out now." He had used a satellite phone to call the authorities at the Department of Natural Resources and they were sending a team post-haste up the hill. Coffey estimated we would meet them in less than two hours, just in time for sunset. All heads were on a swivel. I suspected Coffey was armed, too, but he didn't bring it up. Our pace was steady and the boys chatted comfortably amongst themselves.

Coffey never asked me again why I was carrying a dead body.

Jimbo slipped his hand in mine.

"When I'm sad, mister, Phillip holds my hand. We're not really twins but Mom says we look alike, our hair and ears and nose. So he holds my hand when I'm sad and I think you're sad."

I thought the scouts would snicker at the rambling child, but I was impressed with their inclusion of him, their easy and unforced acceptance. I don't give much credit to teenagers, and this group made me feel petty and small, a lifetime of cynicsm corroding my mind.

Jimbo wouldn't shut up, which was fine with me. It was good to be lost in his world, which sounded busy and productive.

The trek was slow and calming. I could faintly hear Arlo behind us talking to Coffey, likely explaining everything. I was more than fine with Arlo's version of events. It would be hard to fabricate such a tale, and I deserved whatever fate his version assigned me.

Arlo had earned my trust a hundred times over. I didn't believe I had earned his.

I listened patiently to Jimbo and occasionally, Phillip. But I registered nothing. It was difficult to walk, my adrenaline sapping with each step. My arm throbbed, unknown damage that was only calmed by Jimbo's hand curled in mine. Movement brought some peace.

@@@@@

After being checked over for a few hours at the hospital, both Arlo and I were released. Game and Judith were there to greet us, and they had been waiting patiently while the police interviewed us a couple times. Billy would require an autopsy, and I was more curious than anyone to know what the hell happened.

The doctor who worked on the ligament separation or tear in my shoulder wouldn't speculate on Billy's death, but I did tell the doctor that he had a terrible headache the night before. I spoke out loud that it might have been an aneurism, and the doctor said we would know soon enough.

The doctors wanted to keep Arlo overnight, but he had a few choice words for them and said to Game, "No more hospitals for me if I can walk." They gravitated to each other. No one tried more than once to talk Arlo out of leaving.

To avoid thinking I wanted to talk to Judith about the funeral as she drove me home.

"Father Paul told me he'd take care of everything, but that he wanted to have the service quickly. He's scheduled to leave the country and he wants to do this personally." Judith was gentle and direct, as expected. I felt terrible for her, as I knew she loved Billy, too.

But I was not ready to be gracious. "Well, as long as it's convenient for the priest, by all means."

Judith pulled over to the side of the road, despite my protestations and apologies.

"Clem, listen. This is not about you. We are all in shock. We are trying to process it all. No more feeling sorry for yourself, okay?" She put her hand on my shoulder, and if I did anything except say "okay" I believe she would have slapped me.

"Okay."

19

The day of the funeral came fast. No wake, as that apparently was one of the things Billy talked to his friend, pastor Father Paul, about over the years. There would be a mass, a Christian burial, and a post-cemetery reception.

The morning was cold predawn and stayed that way for hours. Clouds moved quickly across the sky as if competing to get out of the way of a larger specter, and today it was the sun, which came through in all its glory just as we arrived at the church.

St. Cosmos is an older parish in a younger area, the neighborhood having been rebuilt through gentrification. The church had the gothic spires and heavy stone that marked Catholicism a century ago. Billy and I rarely spoke of religion in general, but he was a Catholic who was very quick to anger when the subject of errant priests and criminal bishops came up. I always avoided or changed the subject.

The inside was colorful and cool, a magnificent structure that could inspire faith in the faithless. It seemed to stand for all time.

My shoulder pain was softened by the painkillers I was popping like Tic-Tacs, and I felt just fine.

Funny the thoughts that run through your head at the wrong times. As Judith and I walked into St. Cosmos for Billy's funeral mass I recalled when I first met Judith's parents.

@@@@@

Nearly twenty years ago, when Judith and I been dating for a few months, we made the 200-plus mile trek to meet her parents for the obligatory and awkward who-the-heck-are-you dinner. Two weeks after that fiasco her mother died suddenly, a vibrant woman in her prime with many years of love and devotion to her only child, and perhaps grandchildren, ahead of her, married to Ambrose, a certifiable grouch.

Grouch to me only. He liked and was liked by everyone, as Judith tells it. I did not try very hard to win him over, and he saw no need to try at all. Judith and I were serious but not exclusive. I have always worn my selfishness around my neck like a too tight out of style tie, and I had no vision of a future with anyone except myself.

At Judith's mom's funeral, after a week of heavy tears from Judith and Ambrose, silence was their only connection. Ambrose and I sat flanking Judith, in the front row. He was so heavily dependent on his eyeglasses, which were perpetually filthy, that he probably could not see the sun shine at midday.

As the service was about to begin, Ambrose started fumbling with his specs, trying to wipe them off on his suit coat. I instinctively offered my cleaned and pressed handkerchief (for what I presumed would be a torrent of tears from Judith) and he fumbled the glasses. I caught them, and yanked them to me to clean them myself, johnny-on-the-spot.

Ambrose never lost his grip of the glasses, and he pulled and I yanked and he twisted and I twisted and in just a breath the frames were in pieces, irreparable.

The pastor asked everyone to rise, and I was waiting for an outburst from Ambrose, or at least a backhanded slap. It was that bad.

The organist began the dirge. The notes were sad, long, and vaguely identifiable to my heathen ears, and Judith's shoulders heaved. She bent her head. Ambrose bent, too, and his large frame wracked, repeatedly. The mourners behind us audibly gasped, murmured, and hummed, holding back tears, all due sympathy and concern for the widower and the grief-stricken daughter.

Judith and her father were laughing, struggling to keep from outright howls. They never looked up. As they gripped each other tighter, I reached my arm over Judith's shoulder in consolation, the dutiful boyfriend.

She shook me off gently. Father and daughter held each other in waves of suppressed laughter and heaves of giggling grief. I did my best to keep up with the standing, sitting, singing and scripture of the service, as useful as an end table at the beach.

A few years ago Ambrose passed. In the limited contact I had with him he was always civil yet mono-syllabic with me. At his funeral, Judith reflected with little emotion.

"He didn't like you very much," she told me after that service.

@@@@@

Today's organ music stopped abruptly as the closed coffin was wheeled to the front, next to us.

Judith's eyes glistened, turned sad, and she whispered, "He loved you very much, Clem." Then she squeezed my arm tight and burrowed her brow in my shoulder.

I vowed to get through Billy's service without breaking down and I surprised myself with my calm. Principal Myra and her partner, Lillian, sat to Judith's left, with me to her right, closest to the casket.

Marco and his wife and his two adult children sat behind us. He kept putting his hand on my shoulder during the hour, more for himself than for me. I suspect it made us both feel better. I regretted the last time he and I spoke over a month ago, at that dinner where Billy told him off and I was fired and a pawn in Marco's business plans. Regret can be a terrible thing, gnawing and impossible to tuck away. I considered reconciling with Marco today and telling him his presence was important and his friendship over the years had made me a better man. An adversary can be a focal point of initiative and purpose and should be embraced as such.

Poor Myra was having a very rough time. Lillian and Judith alternated hugs and back rubs for her throughout. It was especially intense during the priest's homily, which was short, upbeat, and personal. Brevity was best, and most welcome. Father Paul and Billy went to grammar and high school together, played on the same ball teams and rode the same bus to school. I could see Billy's mannerisms in the priest, an uncanny by-product of people who grow up together.

The priest said Billy was in heaven, and I believed him. "It is too raw right now to appreciate the great good humor of Coach Billy. He lit up the room. He was our friend and confidante. He was generous and outrageous." Father Paul struck a contemplative pose.

"Billy did toil with love. He certainly had no lack of attention and affections. Billy had many admirers, and as devoted a group of friends and acquaintances as a person could accumulate over a lifetime. But he always shared that affection, that love, with others, shared though never committed to only one, an act of unselfishness, it seems. He committed to all his friends and gave everything he had to all of us. And we should ask ourselves, do we give everything we have, in our hearts, to our friends and loved ones?" Father Paul's voice caught, then grew in timber.

"Yet he and me and we are all sinners. In the public place we earn our way to heaven, but our prayers for Billy's soul will help his journey. Yes, pray for him, pray for all the deceased, so that when they sit at the Lord's right hand, all the heavenly hosts can pray for us, the living, and for our salvation, too. Rest in Peace, Coach B. We will miss you."

Then Father Paul sat, and the other people up there, men, women, and children near the altar started their ministrations for the next act of the service.

If Billy toiled with love, I slouched with no self-respect. I was sitting next to the only person who gave everything she had to me, and I treated her like a favorite broken-in baseball glove, worn and battered and useful and an extension of my arm, protecting me while I played and the kind of glove I used exclusively, always had with me, and threw into a corner when I didn't need it.

I was overwhelmingly sad and not a little bit angry – angry enough not to succumb to grief or self-pity. Judith was my soulmate and I needed to make her see that. To make her see, my heart and soul had to change. I just did not know where to start.

The service, the days behind me and the years ahead, started to crash in my ears. A soloist sang gently, real emotion threaded into the music. At one point we were told to say "peace" to each other. Judith and I took cues from Lillian, who knew the rules, and then everyone was hugging and crossing the aisle and crying and more hugging. I stayed stiff, not wanting to offend. Marco bear hugged me and I succumbed to his act of friendship transcending business, at least for today.

From the corner of my eye I saw Arlo midway through the packed church, shaking hands and smiling with my neighbor Game, and then Boo-Boo and several other fit sharp looking dudes and their ladies, probably all vets. Yogi was there, too, with several of their brood, all polished, well dressed, and respectful.

Boo-Boo had so much to be proud of, and I sighed ruefully.

Father Paul touched my shoulder.

"I am sorry, Clem. I loved him, too. He'll be missed and you'll be okay."

I nodded and mumbled something and gripped his hand hard. Marco clapped my shoulder again from behind. Judith crushed my waist and my relief was complete. I had no more tears.

As we filed out of the mass, Judith and I first behind the casket being wheeled out, I tried to keep my eyes front but people, strangers, reached out to touch my arm. Some were just positioning themselves to be seen by Myra and Lillian, which I acknowledged rightly in my cynicism and that brought me no comfort.

Judith dug her nails into my arm and I looked in the direction of her gaze as she locked eyes with an older gentleman, against the back wall, rumpled and disheveled, pepper and salt thinning hair combed straight back, sloppy and askew. The man was grinning, his eyes rheumy and red, nose purpling and pockmarked. A stupid out of place grin.

"Just a bum off the street, Judith," I whispered. "Give him no mind."

Outside, the sun was high and hot, opaque behind gauzy cloud cover. We milled awkwardly as the high school football players turned pall bearers muscled the casket down the steps to the hearse. Myra and Lillian and Judith and I stood in a tight semi-circle on the sidewalk. Marco hovered, rubbing my shoulder every few moments just to make sure we were still functioning and connected.

The funeral director came right up to us.

"Was the service as you wished?" he asked, looking straight at Lillian. She was wonderful working with Father Paul in putting it all together, a thankless task.

"Yes, perfect, thank you." Lillian had an elegance that made everyone gravitate to her.

And to me, he soothed, "We will go the cemetery for a brief prayer, and then we'll return to the parish hall for refreshments. Will that be satisfactory, Mr. Reeger?"

I looked over the crowd. Some began moving to their cars, the funeral home's worker bees handing out fender flags for the short procession. Silent and orderly, people move in shock by rote as we know this can and does and will happen, again and again, when we least expect it.

"Look, friend, Marco Flocario will try to pay the bill. Don't allow it. You're covered, you understand?"

Judith and the other ladies stiffened. I had been harsh and abrupt. I could feel Marco's fingers dig into my collarbone, and the director didn't flinch.

Looking only at me he said, "Of course, sir, I understand." He pirouetted and darted away.

I faced Marco, my chin up in defiance. "Don't go there, man. You can pay for mine." It was my best tough guy line and I nailed it.

Marco smiled through gritted teeth, breathing through his nose. "Okay, my friend. Deal."

There was a commotion of some kind brewing near us, just as the coffin was loaded and the hearse door closed. A bespectacled milquetoast teacher was speaking too stridently to Myra.

"I want his instruction schedule, Myra. And I can coach those teams, too. Better, probably. He was really an asshole, you know."

Myra froze, eyes wide, and Lillian shot a right jab to the gut of that idiot. She stepped into it like a pro. Powerful. Milquetoast dropped to his knees immediately, trying to catch his breath. Unable to cry out, he looked at Lillian and Myra accusingly, pain radiating in his eyes.

Lillian spat at him, "Go to hell, creep." A couple unnamed faces I recognized from the pool of teachers descended on our now prone man and dragged him ungently away.

Lindstrom. I remembered the guy, and he may have been the only person in the universe who bore ill will toward Billy, who understood that Lindstrom's problem was in his own head. I didn't realize teachers could be so rough on each other.

"Nice punch, Lillian," said Judith. "Your hand okay?"

Myra was still frozen. Lillian whispered through clenched teeth, "I didn't give him everything I had." She was breathing heavily, and her composure was starting to crumble.

Marco was at her shoulder, proclaiming, "I saw the whole thing! He fell!"

A crowd developed, straining to get close to hear the conversation, but also attempting to keep a respectful casual distance, with murmurs of agreement to Marco's version of events.

Arlo came up, with Game.

"Man, I haven't been to a Catholic civilian funeral before, but if this is a regular thing I'm gonna get more religious," Arlo said, with Game at his elbow, stifling a laugh.

@@@@@

I should have kept some semblance of bearing at the cemetery, but it was impossible. The enormity of never seeing this good man again, the best friend I ever had and who I did not deserve, came crashing down on my head. Father Paul had everyone say an Our Father and he threw holy water on the casket and then on a small rise about thirty yards away stood Coffey and three of his charge, in full Boy Scout regalia. Phillip and Jimbo stood at attention in crisp salute, while an impossibly thin Scout played Taps, and I lost it. I thought I was done with tears and now it was worse than ever.

Two uniformed Marines folded the flag and Judith accepted it because I couldn't see. I was in a bad selfish place but came around on the short trip back to St. Cosmos after popping a prescribed pill.

Judith and I stuck together through the reception. We were both spent, but we shook hands with everyone in town, even though they didn't know me and I didn't know them. Judith had some celebrity status and half the friends and mourners confessed to having some form of *A Face on the Flag* in their home or office. A surprising number told us they had their picture taken next to it at City Hall. Judith is a gracious sweet sort who truly appreciated the recognition and solidified her kinship with each person who thanked her for it, who told of admiring her work. She could say thank you and mean it and make you glad you took the time to do it.

A newspaper guy asked me if I wanted to comment on Scoutmaster Coffey's version of events from the Crooked Hooker. I did not know what Coffey said to anyone, but I assume he told the police just what he saw and what he did. If not for him, Arlo and I might be dead. Or Billy's remains would have been wild feral pig food.

"No, it's accurate. Now get away from me." I thought I was being charming.

Myra and Lillian stayed in the center of the hall and received a lot of attention. Myra, all boss principal now, was back in control and had applied some makeup and looked refreshed and dignified. Lillian naturally drew a lot of attention, and I glanced her way much too often, thinking her legs ended somewhere under her perfectly aligned cheekbones. The stream of mourners and sympathizers snaked from us to them, and them to us, and within an hour the mood in the parish hall had shifted with a purpose.

The party had started. I noticed people walking about with beer in red cups, and Marco handed me one. Judith declined with a curt head shake. Marco would have his way. He probably avoided Lillian because her meticulous planning for the day would not have included a keg or two of beer.

Father Paul walked up to us, his own red cup in hand. It was half full, and he sipped it for our benefit.

"Nice touch, Marco. Billy would have approved." Marco got away with everything.

"Call me MOFO, Padre."

"Call me Father Paul, my son." And he walked away saluting with the cup. Marco got away with almost everything.

The crowd buzzed louder and seemed to grow during the second hour with no sign of slowing down.

Off to the side of the hall stood Fat Tick talking to an impressively dressed gentleman who I thought I recognized. Fat Tick always dressed well considering his girth, but the other gent, a big man himself, wore formal clothes regally, muted earth tones that covered broad shoulders beneath a chiseled jaw and radiant teeth, with a pencil moustache above a crooked smile, and eyes that took in the crowd in amusement. The stranger had a pose that shouted that he knew he was being looked at intensely and he was comfortable with the scrutiny. He and Fat Tick were talking softly.

"Oh, Clem, look. It's Chuck Chunco, the drummer from *Old Timers* with Fat Tick, my new accountant!" Judith was as giddy as the situation allowed. She caught their eye with a wave and they began to glide through the press of people, two manatees moving through a school of sunnies.

Fat Tick took charge, shaking my hand. "I am sorry, Clem. I understand you were very close. Sorry, Judith." He was all charm, a perfect tone, and eased into an introduction.

"Judith and Clem, I want to introduce you to..." He could not get it out. Judith started pumping Chunco's hand, and then smiles all around. Marco ambled up.

"Hello, Chuck," he said, and they did that back-clap chest bump thing big guys do when greeting.

"Hey, MOFO, good to see you; bad deal, my friend, bad deal." Chunco's concern was genuine.

Chunco started getting a lot of attention then, and the chance to say anything more evaporated. He excused himself and Fat Tick followed in trace. A small herd trailed them outside.

I was impressed. Judith was, too, and then Marco threw in that there must be a motive. I resented his cynicism and told him so. He blew me off and went in search of a refill.

That's when I saw Boo-Boo, standing alone. The casual glare as always, but I double-clutched when we locked eyes. I now remembered about the *Spur* and he thought I did not, and I thought he now might, and a chill went up my spine, and it was fear. It was all in my mind, not his. He gave me a curt and not unfriendly nod and left. The shudder I felt must have alarmed Judith.

"Are you okay?" Judith was still glowing from her brush with a true celebrity.

I told her it was the pain and popped another pill.

We watched the mass of people go from mourners to story tellers, a welcome sight.

Standing against a wall, out of the light, barely visible, was the old grinning guy from the end of the service, alone. I approached him, leaving Judith to a small knot of students.

"How do you do, sir?" I thought I'd be cordial before I kicked him out. He had a plate of food at one point, now an empty plate, and likely a few beers under his belt. I figured him for a local rummy who crashed funerals at St. Cosmos for the free buffet. To each his own but I wasn't feeling magnanimous today. He kept grinning at me. I was prepared to greet him again as if he had not heard me.

He jumped out of a reverie. "Great, thank you." His voice had a rasp to it, a man with a smoking habit or a perpetual cold. I did not extend my hand as his were full.

"Did you know Coach Brown?" My shoulder was acting up.

"Oh, no, I guess not. I do like a good funeral, though." He was still grinning, but my features may have changed enough for him to alter his tone. "Yes, it was beautiful, the mass, uh, Mr..." He coughed.

"Reeger."

"Mr. Reeger. Of course, lovely." I thought I saw recognition in his eyes. "Absolutely lovely. And the crowd, my, my."

"Yes, uh..." I was getting up the nerve to ask him to leave.

"Father Paul had such wonderful words, too. He really felt this one, I could tell. But I do like a good funeral mass. So, Father Paul and the deceased, Coach Brown? They were friends." A statement, not a question.

I softened out of guilt and just plain exhaustion. "Yes, uh, your name, sir?" I tried to smile.

"Jack. Nice to meet you Mr. Reeger." With a dexterity I could not have copied, he shifted his half full beer cup to his left hand with his dinner plate, wiped the free hand on his jacket, and stuck his mitt out for a shake.

I obliged, quickly. "Nice to meet you, Jack. Thanks for being here."

His face now clouded, the affable simpleton grin vanishing with a sigh. "Yes, I'm glad I'm here. Always too late, no?"

I shook my head, blinked, waved good-bye, and walked back to Judith who was listening to several students talking animatedly about a no-doubt Coach B tale. My arrival ended the story and I was finally alone in the crowd with Judith.

"Who is that man?" Judith whispered through a phony smile.

"Said his name was Jack. I think he's just a free food crasher at this church, and the beer is a bonus." I gave Judith's waist a warm squeeze, pressing her hip in mine. She smiled at me, and then I watched Jack walk to the exit, a shadow moving out of the lights, discarding his refuse, nodding politely, and out the door into the twilight. I kept surveying the crowd.

"Let's go, Clem, please. It's been a long day."

"Yes, good, you're right. I was hoping to see another fight..." I looked over toward Lillian and Myra.

"Hmmm. I noticed. You should close your mouth when you stare at her."

"Oh, boy. Sorry."

"No worries, honey. Everyone is. And it looks like your friend Arlo is now on the home team."

Arlo was standing in between Myra and Lillian and the three were chatting it up like old pals. Both women would touch his hand or elbow or forearm or upper arm in what looked like synchronized flirtation, and he appeared accustomed to the attention.

"Good for him." I drained my warm beer and Judith and I snuck out.

@@@@@

We decided to go to Billy's apartment. I had to stay in contact with him, somehow, even if I just sat there. The attorney I was dealing with said Billy had some financial reserves, having been given a head's up through a bank friend, although it was not much at all. He told the court he would handle his estate pro-bono. A real gentleman, he informed me he would provide a more formal detailed accounting of his liquid assets soon. There was no hurry, I told him, as I would make sure expenses would be covered.

"Thanks, Mr. Reeger. Keep receipts..."

"No receipts," I repeated. "Expenses are covered. You let me know."

"Well, then. I understand. I could use your assistance, though. Can you go to his place and give me an inventory of valuables? Everything is subject to probate, I'm afraid, but as he has no family, I am sure there are sentimental items of nominal or no value, and, well, if you could give me a list of what has value. I will trust your discretion and good judgment."

"I got you, counselor. It'll be done this week, and thanks. Thanks very much."

Judith and I walked up the condo flight after unlocking and opening the street level door. This was the second time I had entered Billy's place in all the years I had known him. The first was retrieving the suit two days ago that he would wear forever underground, and that process took me all of four minutes. I could still smell his sweat in the place.

I told Judith just so.

"Never, ever, been here?" She looked at me curiously.

"He was private about that. Odd, right? I always met him in the street or elsewhere."

We were startled when someone started banging on the downstairs door with vehemence. I told Judith to stay there and get ready to call 911. I didn't know what to expect but flew down the stairs with a confidence I didn't feel, heedless of any violence that might meet me. I was spent, angry, and whatever peace I had left I wanted for Judith, for our invasion of Billy's privacy, and for my curiosity.

I threw open the door and barked, "*What?*"

Arlo, his arms spread. "Hey, you guys move fast. I lost you and then figured out where you might be headed."

"Hey, man." I gave him a grin of relief. He returned it.

"Do you mind if I join you?"

We shook hands and trudged up the stairs muttering gibberish, trying to joke, and met Judith at the top.

"Hi, Arlo," she said as they embraced chastely. "What happened? You strike out?"

He shuddered, "Was it that obvious?"

"Oh, yeah." Judith held the "Oh" in exaggeration, widening her eyes for effect.

"I thought I was getting signals, but the friendlier I got the more they backed away. Lillian even whispered to me to back off, but they committed to drinks together soon. I think I'm in love with them." Arlo could have been serious or joking but I couldn't tell.

Judith shook her head. "Keep dreaming, pal."

We snickered without sincerity, and the only thing worse than the silence that followed was the smell of dust, gym shoes, and unwashed dishes.

"How big is this place, Clem? These units don't look big from the outside."

"It is small, Arlo, little bigger than a studio. Kitchen with nook, one bedroom, full bath, oversized dining and living. No half bath. That's it." It came out clinical, like I was selling a loser-space for rent.

Judith flipped on all the lights. The kitchen we stood in was clean, all white, and had the usual stuff. One dish in the sink, probably a sandwich from the night before the hike, or a couple eggs the morning he died. One empty glass; the garbage was empty. Billy would have taken the trash out before a three-day trip.

I looked in the fridge. Spartan. Condiments and seltzer water. The freezer was stuffed full with pro-tein, though, by the looks of it chicken and steak and unmarked wrapped stuff and some frozen veg-etables. I was announcing my findings in a barely conversational voice, the place was that small. I heard no talking from the living room, where Judith and Arlo wandered. The creaks and small groans of footfalls told me they were in different areas, both lost in their own discoveries, the knick-knacks and collectibles of a man's life.

Under a cupboard near the fridge I found an Irish whisky bottle, half full. A fifth of silver tequila comparatively untouched. I didn't announce these, and felt a sharp stab. Billy kept the booze out in the open because it was just for him, no pretense, no visitors.

"Oh, Clement! Oh!"

I darted around the corner, in a lurch. Until that moment I was shaking off the strains and aches and muscle pulls from our time on the Crooked Hooker in stride, shoulder medicine notwithstanding. I felt them all at once at that moment with a too loud, "Ouch, ouch, oh!"

"Are you okay?" Judith's concern was contradicted by her pulling roughly on my sleeve. "Look at this, Clem. Look!"

The wall separating kitchen and living room was a floor to ceiling bookcase filled with books, hundreds of them. Nothing haphazard, well organized, some leather bound, some in covers, many paperbacks, some just old. Every binding had either a large crease or two, or dozens of them. Not one photo on the shelves, though... just books.

Arlo whistled. "Looks like he read them all."

"Look, Clem, *LOOK*!"

Judith's excitement didn't match the scene. "I'm looking, honey, I am. I don't know where to start, though."

She grabbed my arm with both hands and pulled as if trying to save a child from walking in front of a speeding car.

"There! Look!"

My eyes caught leather bound editions of classics, the good kind you buy at Barnes & Noble or through a service that sends you one a month.

Books were Billy's true oldest friends. Teaching, coaching, training at the gym, even occasional binge drinking in self-loathing and pity were just acquaintances. He read all the time, throwing out book title recommendations as a means of unsolicited advice. I hadn't read a book in years, and I felt a pang of sorrow. Billy wouldn't read anymore, his mind lost to the shelves in front of me and the heavens.

"*There.*" Judith's perfect nails dug through my jacket sleeve like the talons of a hawk.

Then I saw it. A three by three-inch square of tin, darkened and splattered by past use and age. It leaned against the leather spine of a Herman Wouk novel, oriented toward the hanging light that shone over the dining room table which looked like Beirut in the 80's. The light fixture cast disparate and weak rays of light throughout the room, though a single stray pinhole shone like a laser beacon directly and deliberately at the tin plate.

I cleared my throat. "Is that what I think it is?" I knew the answer.

Arlo reached for it, and Judith gently stayed his hand. He retreated, unknowing but wiser.

"Jeez, Clem. It looks just like you." He squinted.

It did. I doubted whose mug it was for years, with Judith's silence on the subject as cover. Everyone everywhere always asked her whose face was on *A Face on the Flag*, but she said it was a composite.

"Arlo, I've been looking for this for ages. I thought it was lost in ..."

"Is it from *Face*?" Arlo would not know the details.

"Yes." She sounded authoritative. "Yes, it is. It's the cornerstone, if you will. Except for the door — you know, the one that is hanging – everything else is a copy, touched up. Every poster, t-shirt, post-card, book cover, frat boy flag. All copies. This," and she plucked it off the shelf, "Is numero uno."

She turned it over and brought it up to her nose. "No dust. He just cleaned the shelves."

I was roused to say something profound but all I had was, "Maybe he had a cleaning service."

"Then they do a crappy job." Arlo pointed to corners of the floor, and the coffee table a few feet away. Not filthy, but not clean, either.

Judith dismissed us both. "I can't believe he's had this all this time."

"He probably didn't realize..." I trailed off.

We both knew that Billy understood the sentimental and economic and artistic value. Judith tried to replicate this particular piece dozens of times for a variety of projects and was accused years ago of creating the face electronically with a press of some kind. Judith could replicate the face with pencil points on paper in minutes, and did so on occasion for friends in birthday or milestone cards. The original tin was done with a variety of nails and two different hammers, an agonizing process with frequent failure and several restarts.

Arlo kept staring at me. "I never realized it was your face, man." Then he looked at the tin piece, then Judith, and then settled back on me.

"Neither did I," was all I could manage. Now Judith began crying quietly.

I held her, gently and firmly, a mix of self-revulsion and pride, a swelling in my heart that soothed and that I did not deserve. The *Face* was mine, always was, and I was too blind to see it.

Arlo walked over to the dining table and peered at the scattered and stacked books and papers, discovering a computer setup.

"A laptop. Here's a printer, too, on the floor." He walked around the table, squeezing in the tight space, without looking at us. Judith was uncommunicative, engrossed in her own thoughts. Arlo looked up, and trying to be invisible, he glided into Billy's bedroom.

Judith was back in control.

"Honey, Judith, I..."

"Please, Clem. Don't say anything." She breathed deeply and stepped away from me. "Where's that stupid hanky of yours when I need it?" There was mischief in her voice. She had returned to the task at hand.

I had it out in a flash and she took it and cleared her face up in a couple seconds, in that sweet soft way of being beautiful with nature's gifts of femininity. She smiled and looked up at me with wet eyes and reddened nose. I ached for her.

"I love you, Judith. I do. I'm so sorry about," and I choked, "All of this. Really all of it. I wish..."

She put her hands on my face, leaned forward and up and our noses touched.

"I know, Clem. Me, too. Me, too."

From the bedroom, Arlo spoke. "Not much here, guys." We followed his voice, but not after Judith put the tin impression, her most important creation, back where it was on the shelf.

Billy's bedroom was where he spent his time. Flat screen TV, exercise bike, leather chair and a food tray. The blinds were open and the night view sparkled. I guessed that was why he liked the place. A freakish accident of city planning and architecture gave Billy's bedroom window view a look down a quiet street with a distant spread of a thousand lights where dark and light and color collided into an arresting visual. Simple and beautiful and incongruent, I stared for a moment and then, just as quick, it was simply a well-lit street at night.

"Man, I didn't expect this." Arlo pointed to the bed. It looked like an IKEA twin, maybe a full size, but it was small.

I gazed back out the window, the scene outside sad and melancholy, happiness come and gone.

"We're supposed to inventory valuables. I think we can keep things of nominal value if we want," I said. We looked at each other, hoping someone would take charge.

"Why don't you two take the big room. I can do this," Arlo offered.

"Okay, Arlo. Good idea. But can we do this tomorrow?" squeaked Judith.

We fell over ourselves agreeing with her, settling on 0900. Judith and I were assigned coffee and breakfast sandwiches. Arlo asked if we should invite Myra and Lillian and Judith laughed out loud for the first time since we entered the apartment.

"Let's not, Arlo. It could turn into a circus. We'll pick a few books for Myra and the teachers, maybe donate the whole lot to the school."

"Judith's right, Sergeant. We'll need to cherry pick." I impressed myself with my maturity by not wise-cracking about Myra and Lillian.

"Have you guys done this before? Not for family, but for a friend?" Arlo was speaking from experience and had a way of bringing the situation into focus. "It's harder than it looks. What is important is not always evident. And you keep asking why."

I knew he was no stranger to pain. I suspected he was sticking this out with Judith and me because it was cathartic for him, which was appreciated.

Judith signaled she wanted to leave and stood patiently in the kitchen. Arlo made sounds from the bedroom, a show of drawer slamming, and I slipped a five-spot on the shelf.

Arlo cocked his head at me from the bedroom door, a "come here" gesture of some urgency. I cringed inside. Either he found something disgusting or he witnessed my larceny, and I wanted to avoid a confrontation.

"Hey, Clem. I gotta say this, please just listen." He was anguished. I picked a spot over his left eye and stared at it.

"That pig, the big one I killed. He would have gotten to Billy if we left him."

"Hey, Arlo, you saved us all. You're a helluva shot." I put my hand on his shoulder as he looked away.

"You were right to carry him, Clem. I don't know what I was thinking. Can't leave a man behind. You were right." He took a deep breath and levelled his gaze back to me. "I hope you forgive that."

I was at a loss for words. Almost.

"You were right, Arlo, and you saved us all. That is all that counts. Thank you." I took my hand off his shoulder.

"Clem, you don't get it. I don't get it, either, but what you did was heroic. Truly."

I thought he was patronizing me, yet he was in earnest.

"Really," he continued. "You did what should have been done, the higher difficult solution in the middle of chaos. That's what heroes do, not just react, but to do what is noble and right, what should be done, no matter the personal sacrifice."

"Oh, come on," I tried to interject but he put up a firm hand.

"No, I kept you from falling because I had to, not because I should have. I didn't care about Billy at that point. And I had to shoot that freakin' pig, which was terrifying and thrilling at the same time."

Arlo's eyes were dancing, reliving the moments. He had to save me despite my fear and recalcitrance. Still he stuck with it. Arlo had to shoot that wild boar and he read my mind while I was thinking that the beast would have mauled us. Arlo could be a killer behind those dark eyes but that missed the point. He was a professional well-trained soldier first and last, worthy of the respect he always sought.

"Clem, that pig was never gonna get to us." His eyes were now hard and hollow, the supreme confidence of the battle-hardened survivor. He was substantial and dangerous, the right man in the right place.

Arlo placed a hand on my shoulder. "You earned your Bronze Star, Mr. Reeger, up on that Crooked Hooker. Respect." He nodded as he turned his head away. I resisted the impulse to ask him for more information, to reinforce my curious ego. If I live to be a hundred I would never get a more profound compliment. I didn't deserve it, but I embraced the new warmth in my own skin.

Judith called us from the kitchen breaking the spell.

I opened my arms to her. "Aren't you ready yet?"

We slumped down the stairs, the drain of the day having caught up to us, even Arlo.

I closed the door behind us. "See you at oh nine hundred," and we walked into the cool clean night. I patted my jacket pocket. The tin was where it should be.

20

NOVEMBER 6

J udith spent the night, a big plus, but insisted on staying in the spare bedroom. My charm offensive and offer of a stiff nightcap fell flat. We hugged and she let go first and we retreated to our neutral corners.

I slept like a stone.

The next morning was dreary and wet. Up before dawn, I made coffee and waited for the paper, thinking that Heather would walk her dog after the darkness lifted just a little, admitting to myself that I was a sexist pig and some things wouldn't change. On a whim I called the lawyer's office to leave a message. Two rings and a pickup, quick intro, and I launched into my short speech.

"Hey, hey, hey, stop, stop, it's me." I could hear a loud vibrating hum over his voice.

"Oh, sorry, counselor. Clem Reeger here. I thought I'd leave a message at the early hour, I didn't expect you to answer," I rambled, then in a sprint talking over him, "Good Lord, I woke you! Stupid of me, I am so very very sorry."

"No problem, Mr. Reeger. I'm actually driving to work now."

"Wow. Now I feel really stupid. You must be frightfully busy." I just wanted to dump a message and did not want a protracted conversation.

"I am. All good, though. Beats the alternative. What can I do for you?" The background sound was staticky.

"I need a will. Soon as I can." I tried to sound responsible.

"Right. I understand. If you have loved ones and assets or just good intentions, well, I suspect you're living the confusion now."

"I am. Man, I can't do this to Judith."

"Your wife?"

I sighed. "No. It's complicated."

"When I get to the office I'll text you a couple appointment times. This week is tight. Next week okay?"

I gripped the phone tighter to my head. "Sure, thanks. What do I need?"

"Just bring your last correspondence with data from your financial institutions. Then we'll talk. Just an hour, initially." I think he was trying to write and drive at the same time but I couldn't be sure.

"Okay, I got it. Will do. No problem."

"Be easy on yourself, Mr. Reeger. You've had a tough week."

"Yeah. I have. Sorry about calling with my early morning crisis." I had my eyes shut for no reason.

"No problem. I just billed you for a quarter hour."

I started to say thanks but he had already hung up. I was relieved but kicking myself at the same time. I couldn't let my building anxiety affect Judith.

Creaks from the floor above, a door opening and closing. A few minutes later Judith came down wearing an old sweatshirt of mine, she an infinite beauty I appreciated now more than ever.

"You look like a kid."

She smiled and looked me square in the eye. "I don't feel like one. Is there more coffee?"

I plopped a K-cup into the Keurig machine like I was making an espresso at a great Viennese coffee house. Then she sat and sipped, telling me what she needed and wanted for logistics today, all business, taking her back to her place, turnaround time, getting to Billy's place by nine, connecting the dots.

I couldn't help staring at her.

"And your silence is consent, Clem? Normally you'd be bossing me around."

"What? Who, me?" I would fold on anything, now.

"Do you have a will, Clem?"

"As a matter of fact, I was just talking to the lawyer. And," I needed to be delicate here, since Judith's assets were also substantial. "You need one, too."

"Way ahead of you, pal." She winked, and I was impressed. I leaned closer to her, to hold her hand and tell her I was never going to let her die.

My cell rang. "Yes... Father Paul?"

@@@@@

Our plan for a 0900 meetup with Arlo at Billy's place took a detour.

The Sunshine Diner was a hopping place for a Thursday. Jammed for breakfast and lunch, quick table turn, coffee decent, the homemade pie to die for, and the chow was satisfactory. Judith didn't like the place, so I came for some alone-time meals, which was frequent over the past year. I had not been there since I started training a month ago and felt a pang of misplaced guilt.

"Thank you for meeting me, Mr. Reeger." Jack sat at a window booth and looked like he had been dragged behind a garbage truck, hair akimbo, unshaven, filthy. I was surprised the diner let him in.

I slid into the booth. "It's Clem, Mr. Bowman. I, uh, don't know what to say. Let me start by saying I'm sorry, about your son, Billy."

That grin again, eerie and forced. "Just Jack, Clem. Really. I guess he didn't tell you too much about me, which is understandable, but a way's back he told me plenty about you!"

"Really? Wow, I'm sorry, I..."

"Oh, yeah, many years back, he talked about when you guys were in the Marines. Boy, he bragged about you, decorated war hero, captain of industry, living the life!" The grin was still there and I couldn't gauge his sincerity. Billy did not like him at all, and Jack knew I knew it.

I slumped, and he sagged with me. "I was no hero, Jack."

He stayed silent, staring at my brow.

I stared at my hands. "I got a medal because I was in the right place at the right time. Never pulled my side arm. Never shot at, never in real danger. It's more than humbling; it's humiliating." My knee-jerk annoyance built for explaining it for the hundredth time.

"Oh, now, son. You're being modest." His eyes were soft, paternal and intense.

"No, it's the truth. And if I were ever a captain of industry, well, this captain got fired from the company I helped found." I wriggled my fingers feeling sorry for myself.

The waitress came and took our orders, a king's breakfast for Jack, just coffee and toast for me.

Jack stared at my forehead. "You recognize the waitress?" I told him I did not, and I didn't try to place her in my mind. I was impatient to get to Billy's apartment.

He sighed and shook his head. "She was an altar server at the funeral. Cried the whole time." His eyebrow arched in accusation and for a second my heart tugged. Then I tried to bury it. I had my own problems.

I hoped Jack would fill the silence, but he didn't oblige.

"Look, Jack, the priest told me to meet you. I guess you want to talk about Billy's assets, all that stuff." It came out just short of hostile.

"Well, Clem..." His voice was low, conspiratorial.

I cut him off. "From what I can understand, he's intestate. Last bank statement is less than ten grand, which will take months to sort out, according to the lawyer. His car is paid for, you can have that. Lots of books in his place and not much else. I'm covering the funeral; it's the least I can do."

He tried interjecting at least three times and I kept talking over him. He smacked his hand on the table, twice.

I shut up.

"Clem, son. Stop. Listen to me," his voice just above a whisper.

I sat up straight and inhaled deeply. The food arrived. He had his hands on the table and for the first time I noticed old scars and oversized knuckles, the hands of a brawler. And they were steady, as was his gaze on me.

"I want nothing, Clem. I have weeks, maybe two months, to go. Stage four. Liver."

"Oh, no."

"Oh, yes. Look, do what you think best with Billy's stuff. Father Paul trusts you, then so do I."

"Oh, wow, I'm really sorry." My eyes were still wide.

"Look, son, I like breakfast, especially when someone else is buying. I only have so many left. And I'm hungry, now. I'm gonna eat."

I watched him attack his eggs and bacon, "extra bacon, young lady," he had said. He slurped coffee and chugged juice. The waitress refilled his cup, and I covered mine. I tried giving her a plaintive look of sympathy, but she worked in her own mechanical fog.

"You gonna eat that toast, Clem?"

"Nah, too much butter." I had trouble making eye contact with him.

"Oh, yeah, butter's my middle name. That's the ticket. You mind?" He was cheerful.

We both chuckled as he bit into two pieces slathered with jelly.

"What can I do for you, Jack? Anything?"

His jaw worked like a machine.

"Yeah." He was chewing and did not want to interrupt the tastes with idle chatter. I waited. "Couple things, now that I think of it. Uh, the car. Can you sell it? Pay for my funeral?"

"What? I guess so, I'll..."

"Talk to the lawyer," he finished for me. "Yeah, I get it. And put me next to Billy."

I didn't want to say yes or no. I'd talk to Judith later, but he read my thoughts.

"You'll want to think on that, I'm sure. Billy didn't tell you much about me, but he told me about you, his best buddy. You don't owe me crap, son. But you'll do the right thing."

I sighed, deep and long. Exhaling, "I will."

"Right." He swirled a piece of rye toast around the plate, sponging the last drops of grease and egg he could scrounge. He scraped so hard he might have gotten elements off the plate from meals a year in the past.

"One other thing, Clem. I'd like to go to his apartment, have a look around."

I gave up. "Sure thing." I would have caved on anything, and this seemed a small thing to allow.

"Soon, okay?" That outsized grin.

"Let's go now," I said. It was my first chance to be decent, having regrettably dragged Billy's disrespect for Jack into this contact.

He clapped his hands, loud, and most of the patrons in the diner jumped. "Splendid! Pay the bill, my boy, and let's ride!"

Jeez. It sounded like Billy.

We arrived at the condo uneventfully. Jack and I walked from the kitchen to the living room and he stared at the dining table cluttered with paper for a long moment. He stuck his head into the small bedroom, focusing on the nightstand and the tallboy bureau of drawers.

"No photos, nothing." He sighed.

"No, sir. One picture, out in the living room."

Jack scratched the top of his head and flakes of dandruff and crud popped up and fell. "Not one of his Mom. She was a good gal, really. Gone too soon. I gave them both a reason to hate me."

Another short sigh which he caught in his chest, and the exhale came out in a loud dry sob. I reflexively touched his shoulder, and he patted my hand.

"He came out real good, huh, Clem Reeger? A good man, right?"

I was fighting my own tears. I swallowed hard, twice. "A great man. The best."

I showed him the lone picture, a group shot, relieved that I had not taken it home myself yesterday. Billy, Judith, me and about a dozen people singing in a bar, taken about ten years ago, neighbors and friends far down the spectrum of time. He held it and smiled and gave it back to me without a glance. Jack was eye-balling the bookshelves.

"Impressive. I knew he liked to read. I used to read a lot. I was hiding from my family, sometimes in plain sight, until I couldn't hide anymore. So, I just left them. Say," he paused, perhaps waiting for me to question or comment, or frozen by the memory of his abandoning the only people who ever had a glimmer of faith in him. "There's several gaps here, and here, and... Did you take anything?"

I silently gagged. I had taken something, the tin plate of my face that Judith had looked for, for years, that fell into Billy's hands somehow long ago. I kept my mouth shut.

"Oh, no matter. I want nothing. I have no claim to anything, no desire, really," he trailed off in a whisper.

"I understand, Jack, I do."

"Look, son, we have a deal." He stared at me, for the first time a hard look on the border of menace. Then his focus shifted.

"Well, looky here, Clem. A five-dollar bill. Right here." He picked it up, holding it aloft as I held my breath. "Uh, do you, mind?" he said with a smirk.

"No, no, no, that would be fine. I was going to do an inventory later today, and if I find any other cash..."

He waved me off. "No, that will settle accounts, as they say. Now, back to arrangements. We have a deal, right?" The same hard edge was back.

"Yes, yes, we do."

All business. "Good. We can go now. Take me back to the diner. I'll walk from there."

"But, how, uh, will I get in touch?"

"You won't. Nothing personal, Clem, really. I have my own people. You wouldn't like them." He gave me that forced grin, which I now saw as maniacal.

"Wait, Jack. You stormed into my life and now you're just going to vanish?"

He coughed and chuckled at the same time, yet got serious in a flash. "This ain't about you, Clem. None of it is. Father Paul will call you when the time comes. Do your job, then. We have a deal."

I drove him back to the diner in silence. Then I called Judith that I would pick her up to go back.

@@@@@

The sun broke through about 1000 and it brought the cold air with it, crisp and clean, inviting us to get inside. Arlo arrived at Billy's condo the same time we did.

We milled about the small space, ignoring each other as best we could when bumping is inevitable, like being in the bestseller aisle at a bookstore. Lost in our own thoughts I took mental notes. Arlo and Judith were more conscientious, jotting things down. I predicted in my mind that we would just throw our hands up and donate all of it, after cherry picking an item or three. Then my promise to the lawyer about an inventory came roaring back in my mind. I sighed audibly.

"What's the matter, Silly?" Judith was as sweet as ever. I shook my head at my fortune.

I already had my prize, and her smile never failed to take my breath away.

"Clem, did you see this?" Arlo, kneeling behind the dining table, was holding a thick sheaf of papers.

"See what?" I walked over and took the bundle from him.

The cover page was brand new.

Bed Bug Stew
Stories by William J. Bowman

On white bond paper, double spaced, close to two inches thick, was what appeared to be a manuscript. Two hundred thirty-six pages. I thumbed through it unsure if I understood what it was.

I whistled while Arlo stood and I showed it back to him.

"Yeah, that's really cool, I know." We both strode into the kitchen.

"We found gold, Judith." We stood gawking at each other. Judith's hands shot to her mouth.

"Holy cow. I didn't know. Did you?" She was drifting somewhere between joy and incredulity, a happy place for a child but uneven and wild for an adult.

"I want to read it right now," she said, unable to conceal her excitement. By now Arlo was fiddling around with the laptop.

"Man, I hope he has this somewhere," tapping keys and opening hutch drawers at the same time, rifling though it gingerly. "Here! A flash drive. Unmarked. Right on top. I'll save it in case we can't open this sucker."

The laptop sprang to life and asked for a password. "I don't suppose you kids know his password," beseeched Arlo.

"Try Judith," I said impulsively, and Judith rejoined with "Try asshat!" And we three laughed.

"Well, I did the all zero thing, so I think I'll try," and he started typing. "Bingo!"

I looked at him stupidly, and said the obvious, "His password is bingo?"

He made an exasperated snort. "No, Marine, it's semperfi."

Arlo went through word docs and found a ton of drafts and poetry and the building blocks of the semi-completed hard copy work of *"Bed Bug Stew."* We played with the files without being intrusive, Arlo using an unspoken logic of dates and prefixes that is easy for that generation. We began printing single pages of bills and financials, as few as practical. I knew this would be helpful and valuable for the lawyer.

There was nothing else extraordinary. We stayed away from emails for the time being. I could not go that deep yet and considered if it was an invasion.

Judith had settled into the couch and was reading the manuscript.

"Wow. Fascinating. And this came from Billy. It looks like a novella and a series of short stories.

Maybe you should check his email. Maybe he had an agent or a publisher or somebody might own this, right now. A problem." She never took her eyes off the material.

I was torn between happy and sad. "A very nice problem to have. Billy has left the world more than just good will and great friends. He has left something that can be remembered with exactness, better than a trophy. Better than any trophy at all."

Arlo asked me what time it was. I was a little annoyed, as the wall clock was behind him and easy to see with little effort. Then I was inspired. I took off my Rolex and told him to take it. I expected a little pushback, oh-I-can't-possibly, but he never hesitated, putting it on his wrist and staring at it.

"Thanks, Clem. This is the nicest thing I've ever worn." His smile made me feel ten feet tall.

It took less time than we thought, finishing a decent inventory of everything in less than 90 minutes. Judith was no help at all and read Billy's book or whatever it was the whole time. Arlo had a genius suggestion that we simply photo objects and video the bookshelves. The real value was the manuscript and we knew it. We tidied up a great deal, stripped the bedding, wiped down surfaces and Arlo ran a vacuum.

"I'm done for the day. I'll review everything with the lawyer today or Monday and we could box up over the weekend." I was starving, Arlo grunted approval, and Judith expressed hunger for the first time in days.

We drove separately to Jersey Mike's, a favorite for all of us. Judith talked the whole time, telling us about Billy's collection of stories, one after the other. Even though I am not a big reader I couldn't wait to get my hands on it, too.

Once finished with lunch Arlo went his way after much warm hugging and self-congrats all around. I was starting to feel alive, forgetting for a moment the end of seeing Billy everyday. I tried to take another pill and got the fisheye from Judith. We opted for holding hands on the ride for comfort.

We settled into my kitchen, and Judith expressed displeasure at the contents of my fridge, volunteering to go shopping at that moment. I begged off, and she shook her head.

"You're not invited. We can only buy so many cookies, Clem."

As Judith was walking out the door, my cell rang. It was Marco.

"How are you holding up?" Marco probed, and I asked him the same.

"Hey, Clem, I know this is coming out of left field, but this Chunco guy, who I barely know, asked me if Billy left any, uh, you know, papers. Like a book or a manuscript. I said I had no idea and that you were doing the necessary walk through of Billy's place and all. I told him I'd ask you, and..."

I didn't hear much after that. Perhaps he stopped talking. Chunco? He was a real player, and he knew Billy? And the book? I came back to earth.

"Marco, it's sitting in front of me. On my kitchen table. And there's a copy on a flash drive. Judith has read much of it already, and I was going to spend the rest of the day with it." My voice caught a couple times.

"Clem, why don't you call this guy direct?" He gave me Chunco's number. He inhaled loudly. "Hey,

Reeger. We're good, right? I have been less than..." he trailed off.

I gave him my best vulgar DI expletive, called him MOFO recklessly, and I could hear laughter on his end. "Yes, you fat slob, we're good." I meant it. We hung up.

I wanted to speak to Fat Tick first but didn't have his number. I dismissed calling Chunco out of the gate, not because I harbored suspicions, but because I wanted to know if there was value with the manuscript. I had to report the book to the lawyer. I knew who to call, then, and did so with Arlo's admonition in the back of my mind. I hit the number, hard.

"Hey, Boo-Boo, how the heck are you?" I know I sounded much too confident and cheerful. As soon as he spoke I thought this might be a mistake.

"Well, well, Clem. Good of you to call. I was going to reach out myself, maybe on Saturday."

I couldn't see him, yet I assumed he was hunched over his desk, leaning into each word, being intimidating in my imagination. I threw the whole thing out to him in a rush, finishing with a request for Fat Tick's number.

"Why do you assume I have it?" He was even keeled, too much so.

I responded with silence. I almost hung up, my heart was thundering so bad.

Boo-Boo sighed. "I'll text it to you."

I was profuse in my thanks and wanted to get off the phone.

"Clem, you did the right thing calling me. Not about the book. I am truly sorry about what happened. You did the right thing, all around, according to Arlo and Coffey. You done good, Marine."

My throat caught for the second time that day. I tried to say thanks, but I choked out, "You know Coffey?"

Boo laughed, the genuine booming laugh I had grown to enjoy. "Clem, everyone knows Coffey. Great people, one of my guys. Good luck with the book thing. Don't be a stranger." And he hung up.

I sat for a few minutes and waited for the number to be sent, staring at the second page of the manuscript, which had a brief dedication: *For K. S.*

I had no idea who that might be and wracked my memory for the combination of initials. Judith might know.

When I got Boo's text, I called Fat Tick right away. He gave me a big hello, and a bigger "sorry" again, and said he knew why I was calling. Only he didn't sound like the mythical Fat Tick, destroyer of all the air in the room and the women at his feet. He sounded like an accountant, which he was. I smiled goofily just thinking about him wearing a green eye shade.

I told him what we found and he asked the appropriate questions. I had to interrupt him, though, to ask why he was interested.

"Clem, Billy and Mr. Chunco hit it off a couple years ago when his step-son, Scott, was playing ball at school. When Chuck Chunco makes the scene it creates a scene, and he needed some alone time talking to the coach about the boy and the team and playing time. You know, dad stuff. Good kid, too."

"I know Scott Spaeth, actually met him a couple weeks ago. Did some, uh, work for me at the old firm." I tried to sound business-like and on top of it all. "Yeah, very mature, personable young man."

"Yeah, he's joining the Navy. Mr. Chunco is not happy about that. Anyway, they met twice, got to talking and solving the world's problems, and Billy tells him he writes stories. Mr. Chunco said he wanted to see his work, but Billy told him it wasn't ready. Apparently, they started talking again on the phone just over the last month, seems like Billy got a burst of energy and polished it all up. A week ago, Billy tells Mr. Chunco the manuscript is ready, and he would deliver it in hard copy after the weekend hike."

Stunned, I gasped out loud.

"Yeah, I know. Mr. Chunco is now really interested. He was only going to encourage and maybe coach him a little through the circles of agents and such in publishing, but now he is compelled. Mr. Chunco does not have a legal right, Clem, but he, well, wants to get this done now, in a big way."

Fat Tick had a melodic cadence like he could have been a minister in his own right. I focused on three things. First, the constant formal reference to Mr. Chunco, as I assumed that everyone bowed to Fat Tick, not the other way around.

Second, that my unavailability to raise hell at night during my month of "training" kept Billy at home, too. To write. It was almost too much to bear.

Third, that Billy's manuscript could be his legacy and that October had been our destiny.

We are all put here on earth possessing a wide array of talents, hopes, and dreams, and sometimes those dreams do come true, because of tons of hard work and a little luck. I slouched through my life and was surrounded by people of substance: Billy, Boo-Boo, Arlo, Fat Tick and Chunco, Game, Coffey and his Boy Scout troop, poor Steve Spaeth and his progeny, Scott. And of the most important person, a real artist of stature, my Judith. These were all substantial people of accomplishment, whose lives were professional, ordered, and they took complete responsibility for their own successes and failures and likely never once blamed someone else for bad results.

Why would anyone associate with me, a slacker of the highest order? "What did I do to deserve being surrounded by heroes?"

"Maybe we just like you, Clem. You're genuine."

I swallowed hard and tried to hide a phlegmy cough.

"Did I say that out loud?" I was mortified, but I was talking to Mr. Tiggiero, an accountant.

"You did, my friend, but I think it was meant for yourself. Be at peace. Life really is wonderful and it will go on," he said, as gently as a man can speak to another. We listened to each other breathe.

Fat Tick told me that the *Old Timers* were going to open Thursday Night Football tonight on TV, and to make sure I caught it. He then gave me instructions for the flash drive, to make a copy and tell the lawyer about the conversation.

"Keep the hard copy of *"Bed Bug Stew"* you have, Mr. Reeger. You've earned it."

@@@@@

The lawyer called. A doctor friend had relayed to him that the preliminary autopsy on Billy was a massive brain aneurism. "He never knew what hit him." A toxicology report would take weeks, but I knew that would be clean.

Judith and I mused on that, a little closure in a wound that would never completely heal.

We ordered pizza for dinner, just like back in the day. We were a couple again, I think, without saying so. We had gabbed all afternoon, without sulking in grief. She finished the manuscript and I started it, but Thursday Night Football needed the proper preparation and we began our happy hour in anticipation.

I always thought a woman who loves football is a keeper. It was time to act on it.

I set *"Bed Bug Stew"* aside. I had everything to say to her and nothing prepared.

Judith interrupted me before I could start. The preview of *TNF* was coming on, and the *Old Timers* were on a massive stage, a taped event. The crowd was frenzied and the camera showed them all, Chuck Chunco prominent, playing the drums without effort, and the rest of the band members had individual closeups, all happy and engaged professionals and friends. Another camera panned the front row of people, and there was Scott Spaeth and his Mom, who seemingly never aged at all, along with Fat Tick, who looked much the same, and kids of a wide variety of shapes, sizes, colors, and ages.

Everyone was singing the words to an Eagles classic, *Take It to the Limit.*

> *"You can spend all your time making money*
> *You can spend all your love making time*
> *If it all fell to pieces tomorrow*
> *Would you still be mine?"*

And we found ourselves mouthing the words, too. The *Old Timers* were pitch perfect and harmonized beautifully, bringing back wonderful memories of us, of Billy, of coming of age together. Yet something was missing.

The song ended, and the blasting promo of crashing helmets and battle and martial combat commenced. A real buzz kill.

Judith grabbed the remote and tried to work it. "Please kill the sound, Clem." I did.

"You know, the lyric: *"You can spend all your love making time"* just seemed to fit the rhythm, the tempo of the song," she whispered. I murmured agreement.

"But that's not it," she said gently. "You see all those children in the front row, singing? That's their family. All their kids and wives and husbands and besties. People who love each other have children, and they created time in the process. Time marches on, but children perpetuate time. The whole cycle, from birth to adulthood and finally..."

I was impressed with her depth. "I think it's too late for us to have kids, Judith," I said, with a soft gaze that begged for her understanding that I loved her and I could not talk yet about death.

She nodded, resigned. "Oh, I know, Silly." We sat watching the kickoff.

"Judith, baby, we can't create time. But isn't your art your time? It has its own immortality. Isn't that enough?"

She touched my face now, a mix of love and sadness in her eyes. I held my breath and my tongue, and she didn't have to say it. I had no legacy, no time. I had spent my life, my time, making and spending money. Billy, the man of a thousand best friends, had achieved a certain everlastingness. Surely the *Old Timers* created their own immortality copying the work of others and everyone loved it. Their work honored time and they created time itself with the existence of their families.

I could not get Billy out of my mind. I knew I was not ready for the hereafter myself because I was certainly not ready for Billy's sudden death. I did not understand or give hard thought about chance and time and God and what will not come to be no matter how hard I planned for it. Or how to turn back the hands of time to redeem myself to Judith or bring back Billy. I resolved to be better about my life, to appreciate and enjoy God's gift to me, a woman who loved me. I would make myself ready.

"Judith, I want to go to Madison with you. As your husband or boyfriend or paramour or cabana boy, I don't care. I love you, I want you, and we'll buy extra socks and long underwear." I wanted to be both cute and serious. We have had similar conversations in the past and they always throw her for a loop. I held my breath. "Besides, I'm out of work." I gave her my best idiot smile.

"Good." She squeezed my hand.

I saw that it is never too late to do the right thing, action which is invariably arduous and fraught with contradictions, falsehoods, and disappointments. All the trials of life are placed at our feet by unseen elements, by God or fate or cruel coincidence. I had spent my life letting circumstances control my action or inaction. I always took the easy way out. I never took responsibility for doing what was right and good, first. I treated the people who treated me best as accessories to my own selfishness.

I never took a chance to be great at anything. I probably wouldn't, either, at this stage.

I decided to be happy. "Let's pack, Judith."

21

Game drove into the mall parking lot as the sun crested over a red cloud behind the silhouette of the building, before the lunch crowd developed and the donut shop slowed down.

Arlo was standing by his truck, arms folded over his chest, his North Face jacket not quite up to the task of keeping him warm. He approached Game's car with more bounce than usual.

Their vehicles were both shoe-horned into a small section by dumpsters since much of the main parking lot was cordoned off for repair. Four hard edged and sharp toothed bucket plow machines were staged at the four corners of the lot, facing at angles, ready to tear and grind up the asphalt. Large grading machines were on deck to smooth out the surface after the fun work of destruction was finished.

Game called out while approaching. "Should be a two-day job, if they hustle. Rain's gonna hold off, I think."

"Hi, Dad. Thanks for coming." Arlo stuck out his hand which Game ignored, who moved in for a bear hug.

"Damn, I am so very proud of you son," Game half-whispered, eyes moist.

"I know, Dad. I have been, well, wrong about so many things." They stood a foot apart, staring at their toes. "I am not a victim, I never have been. I know now that I can't let old grievances get in the way..." Arlo trailed off.

"Forget it, son. Thanks for spending so much time with me this past week. I must say I was a lonely man." Game inhaled deeply and held it. "I know the whole ordeal must have been awful." Game kept a firm hand on Arlo's shoulder.

"You know, I just don't think I can handle too much more of that, but I gotta tell you, this spare part," and he tapped his prosthetic foot twice on the ground, "is starting to kill me."

Game grimaced more than Arlo. "The VA will get you a new leg, won't they?"

Arlo shrugged. "Yes, but it will take time. I want the best one they make, and I have a few friends in low places who might be able to help."

Boo-Boo broke the private conversation by shouting from the storefront. "Your vehicles aren't that nice to park so far away. C'mon in!" He beckoned to Game and Arlo.

"You know what he wants to talk about?" Game suppressed annoyance.

"Oh, yeah. Clem Reeger wants to bring *Heroes Who Hike* up to Wisconsin. Boo wants to know if he can hack it on his own," Arlo said, noncommittally.

Game squared his shoulders. "He can."

"Dad, Clem thought I was the client for the hike." Arlo arched an eyebrow.

Game laughed, and said, "Yeah, I know. Coach B was pretty slick setting it all up. Freaky that his plan wound up, well, you know." He bowed his head. "Clem worked hard to get ready. Kept him going at the right time. And if not for Billy's help..."

They stood in silence. Arlo broke it by saying, "I agree. He can hack it. But I hope the hills are smaller up there, for his sake."

In a soft voice, Game said, "Arlo, I know I wasn't there for you; your mom and I just couldn't."

It was Arlo's turn to put an arm over Game's broad shoulders. "That's all in the past."

"I know, son. I just want you to know how sorry I am, how sorry I have always been." Game stopped and hugged Arlo again.

The construction equipment all fired up at the same time, a deafening chorus.

"You'll never be lonely again, Dad."

THE END

Acknowledgments

I have been writing this novel off and on for nearly three years since I retired from full-time employment. I had a loose plot line and interesting characters that I wanted to share and thought the effort worthwhile. The biggest hurdle was balancing too many projects, which is a classic mistake. I learned my lesson.

I had a lot of help getting this over the finish line. My son Dan (Navy vet) and my brother Matt read the nearly completed manuscript and offered crucial corrections, observations, and advice. I could not ask for more devoted people to be straight with me in all respects, and it is a better work because of them. Ray Thompson (Army vet) and Mark Hauck (USMC vet) assisted with specific counsel on areas that required more expertise, and Greg Malacane touched on numerous elements of writing style that needed polish. I cannot thank these people enough for their time and assistance.

A big shout out to the generous endorsers who gave "Advance Praise" reviewing the almost completed version, and for Xulon Press for making this come together.

Last and most importantly, half of all royalties for this work, as with my previous two historical novels, will go to charities, foundations, and support groups for veterans. I have been blessed to have given away many thousands of dollars to noteworthy organizations dedicated to veteran care and support. For a full run-down of those charities that are solid and that I recommend for your generosity, please visit my website at www.kevinhorganbooks.com.

To all my friends and supporters, readers and fellow writers, thank you, again and again.

Memento Lapsos Bellator:
Remember the Fallen Warrior.